A Minotaur Tale

Being a Monster Romance for Yuletide

Kass O'Shire

Contents

To people with religious trauma surrounding
the holidays,
Here's a cinnamon roll minotaur, hope it helps.

A Note from the Original Author

THE EVENTS OF THIS work take place prior to the removal of the Lady's Barrier, specifically in the Year Post Slumber 979. My intent is to show the citizens of the Compact of Nations how others live in the rest of the world in a way that feels accessible and amusing. If you would like more concrete facts about the peoples that have long suffered under the regime of the Pathain Empire, or those of the town of Sanctuary, please see my other scholarly works or those cited in the footnotes. All of my stories are crafted around stories told to me by those that lived them with their express consent, and any deviations from the truth are meant to entertain, and have been approved by the involved parties. I will add footnotes to clarify details as needed, but my intent is that these should be treated as one might a work of fiction.

   -Sirin Agbuya-Broderson YPS 1012

Chapter One

IN WHICH LIBRARIES ARE SACROSANCT, MINOTAURS ARE VEXING AND THE HOLIDAYS APPROACH

"**I**S THAT FOOD? DID you bring *food* into my library?" Cora shrieked.[1]

"No, they're cookies, they ..."Asterion trailed off. His bovine ears drooped, and she almost felt bad for yelling at him. Almost. Until, of course, she remembered that he brought *food* into her library.

---

1. Never mind the fact that shrieking was also against the rules of her library, but food, of all things, merited a special dispensation.

"Cookies. Are. Food." Cora was quickly approaching the end of her patience with this man.

Perhaps minotaurs had especially thick skulls, because, for some reason, Asterion couldn't seem to get it into his head that she wasn't interested.

Well, she supposed, that wasn't *strictly* true. If she wasn't who she was, she would absolutely be interested. The man was gorgeous, tall and broad with short, messy hair that made him seem debonair and boyish, despite the fact that he was a revered diplomat. From what she'd seen in books and illustrations, Cora had assumed they'd have a body covered in fur, and a more cattle-like head, but Asterion's was more of a suggestion of a bull. He had horns that were annoyingly adorable and a flattened nose that was still distinctly bovine, but he had fairly humanoid looking lips.

Below the waist was where he truly differed from other humanoids. He had fur covering his legs that were hocked like one would expect, and a tail that hung beneath the short skirt of his chiton. After watching him walk away one day, she'd decided that the combination was dangerous on a man, between the flowing fabric, the strong legs, and the tail that swished behind him, he could melt anyone's heart.

She'd caught herself staring far more often than she'd liked. He had hooves of course, that clicked in the entrance to the library, so he always knew when he'd arrived and the second he was leaving, even though she didn't care to know either way. So yes, given the right circumstances, she was sure she would be interested in him.

Regardless, he would surely not be interested in her—not if he knew her–and therein laid the problem. He spent entirely too much time in her library, distracting everyone with his good natured attitude and devastating looks.

"You need to leave. You need to take your cookies and get out of my library before you damage any books."

"But they're Madeleines, they —"

"I don't care, they could be made of solid gold and you would still need to leave."

He left then, blowing air out of his nose in annoyance, and Cora felt a tiny twinge of guilt that he looked so dejected, but she'd seen this story before. Once Asterion, and his food, were gone, Cora helped a selkie and an orca-shifter find some information on bonds. After that, she spent a largely normal day in the great library of Berggeheimnis. She reshelved books and typed up late notices on her typewriter, to be sent out via messenger. The significant influx of new residents to the city meant that Asterion wasn't the only patron she was having to acclimate to the rules.

He'd arrived in the city amongst several hundred others, as his people's representative to the newly formed, but as of yet unnamed, clandestine rebel opposition government. For centuries, the dwarves of Berggeheimnis had hidden in their mountain home, maintaining a decrepit village above ground to trick the elves of the Empire into thinking they were on the verge of dying out.

Instead, the city housed a massive population of dwarves within a massive cavern, watched over by a settlement of dragons on its peak.[2] Its history meant it was the perfect location to begin the delicate process of unifying the disparate peoples of the Empire in hopes of freedom.

For Cora though, it was overwhelming. Her city, which had once made so much sense to her, was flooded with newcomers, and she'd spent less and less time roaming the city than

---

2. For those unfamiliar, Berggeheimnis refers to both the city and the mountain which houses it. Situated on Caihalaith's eastern shore, the city was housed in a massive cavern and had access to land, sea, and air, via it association with the dragons that roosted on it's peak and the cove hidden amongst it's rocky cliffs.

she was wont to do, simply because it was so *loud*. Seeing all of the different peoples was fascinating, especially as she'd read about so many of them, but they all had different mannerisms and social norms... and most days she felt she barely knew what to do in dwarven society. Even the mountain seemed fine with all of the hubub, excited even, so she was quiet alone in her bother.

But in the library? She knew the rules, she *made* the rules, so at least there, she felt safe.

When all of her pertinent tasks were done, she was grateful to find she had some time to settle with a book of her own. The library had recently acquired a new shipment of books including, to her joyous surprise, a natural history text about the marine life of the southern coast of Caihalaith. Being tied to her mountain as she was, she would never see a coast other than the rocky cliffs just outside and the cove that made up the hidden port of Berggeheimnis.

There were worse places to be trapped, she knew. In the grand scheme of being a nymph, she was lucky. Instead of a tree or flower she was tied to an entire mountain, one that housed an underground city, no less. She could roam anywhere within its borders, but she'd never be able to leave. Instead of a tree or flower that could die, ending her life, her mountain was old, enduring and wise, a constant source of comfort and stability. She reached out to it then, attempting to draw comfort from it's steadfast nature.

The niggling sense of unease that she'd had at Asterion's visit was difficult to shake, however. The minotaur came most days the library was open, often in the afternoons when he was done with his business on the council for the day. He read widely, not that she paid much attention to the books her patrons checked out or pulled from the reference section. At first, he'd done what appeared to be a survey of the many peoples that lived in the Empire, and therefore the many cultures now represented in the city and on the council. Then, he touched on history, including spending hours pouring over forbidden texts that couldn't leave the library and needed special dispensation to read. It had taken him months, but no matter what she said, what she offered by way of summarization, he'd been determined to read it all himself.

Cora had disliked Asterion from the start. He was loud and messy, had seemingly no idea how to compose himself in a library, and had a smile that somehow melted her indignation if she didn't nurture it closely. He'd bow his head and blush, rub his hocked hoof over the floor in chagrin and all of her righteous fervor would drain. One minute she'd be waggling her finger, whisper-admonishing him, and the next she'd be calmly explaining the rules and trying not to giggle at his self-effacing jokes.

In short, he was the perfect kind of torture. Someone she *should* easily detest, yet she could never quite muster the ability. His consistent offers to help around the library, his smiles and blushes when he'd broken a rule, interfered with her ability to feel as she ought, no matter how she tried.

Unfortunately, as was often the case—despite her careful study—it took her quite some time to realize he was flirting with her. He'd asked for his usual study cubby and as much as Cora would have liked to let him go by himself, it was absolutely against the rules. Cora had staff at the library, of course, but they were mostly students who arrived after their classes were done for the day. She had them accompany Asterion whenever possible, but on that specific day no one was available.

She'd walked him from the front desk, through the tall stacks of the first floor while he babbled on behind her.

"It really is such a magical place though. All of these books, and I can't even imagine how you keep them all organized. I'd have them all over the place, or better yet, locked up tight. And *this—"* he'd gasped when they arrived at the elevator, like he'd never ridden in them before. "It's just *genius*, who'd have thought of devising a system of tracks and catwalks for the second floor so you could see all the way to the roof? Not me, I wouldn't think of such a thing, I'll tell you that!"

He whipped his head around as they walked, and Cora had worried that he'd move it too quickly and those massive horns he sported would snap his neck. And where would she be then? A death in the library was just too much to even contemplate, let alone dealing with the death of a foreign diplomat! Worse yet, who would she get to help her put books on the highest shelves? She'd have to go back to using a ladder and moving it from shelf to shelf was so *tedious.*

"Do be careful with your horns," she'd interjected into his stream of admiration, annoyed that she even had to consider such a thing.

"Oh, of course," he'd quieted then, which was an altogether unsettling experience, looking so disappointed in himself that Cora, in turn, felt guilty.

"The library was designed by Curin Bronzebart, the famous architect, as a wedding present for his wife, based on a fanciful idea she'd had about mine carts that could be used to deliver books."

Asterion whistled in awe, eyes roaming the stacks as they ascended. He gasped then, drawing her attention, and she followed his gaze to the third floor... and her apartment.

"Did they live up there?" his voice raised, as it often did, to a wholly unacceptable-in-a-library volume. He pointed a massive arm, of *course* with the arm free from his draped garment, highlighting the delicate furring of his chest and the brown nipple it flagrantly displayed.

Cheeks hot, Cora snapped her head to the cart controls, as if she'd find life's answers hidden there. She squeaked an affirmative answer, and hoped he'd drop the subject. They *had* lived there, but she wasn't sure she could handle knowing he was thinking about *her* current residence, she'd simply die of mortification.

"What a wonderful idea... what a gift..." he mused, eyes roaming once more.

Asterion kept quiet as she steered them to his cubby and was just about to leave him, when he spoke again. "You're so lucky to work someplace so *beautiful*," he said, but he looked at *her.* He placed his hand on hers, gently, as if she were a skittish animal he was afraid to drive away."I do wonder though, if you ever leave... to go out to eat, perhaps?"

The eye contact, the heat where his hand touched hers, and the *question* collided in a roar that had assaulted her entire being. Heat pulsed from where he touched her and she felt herself immediately blush. He was *flirting* with her, it had just taken her too long, again, to realize it.

It was a common problem, with her being a nymph, she received more overt passes regularly. The subtler ones though, often eluded her as her mind seemed ever so slightly out of lockstep with everyone around her. As a child, raised lovingly by a family of dwarves, she'd assumed that she looked at the world differently because she was not a dwarf. And while that was likely at least partially true, her subsequent experiences with other beings, nymphs especially, led her to believe that there just might be more to it.

As a nymph, Cora was cute and seductive. Her white skin was marbled with gold and accented with beautiful gems, not wholly representative of the mountain rock of which she'd been formed, but of her mother's desires for her instead. While she was perhaps plumper than some peoples' tastes, she had grown up in the dwarven city of Berggeheimnis and followed their shape. As she'd never left the underground city, nor would she ever be able to, she'd been glad to blend in where she could. As a child, the library had been a refuge for her, a place where she could escape and explore the places that she would never be able to, and escape the noisy overwhelm of the city. She'd worked hard to become head librarian at twenty-six, and she couldn't afford to be distracted by the heartache that would inevitably follow any attempt at romance.

Coming of age had introduced further difficulties, as she learned that many nymphs were often polyamorous and regarded as being free, easy, and fleeting with their affections. While she wasn't averse to friendship or romantic entanglements, she found that she sometimes had difficulty forming connections, and that others expected her, by virtue of her race, to be easily wooed and easily left. Often, she'd not realize that someone was trying to get her romantic interest until they were quite forward. If she found herself interested, one of two things would happen. She'd quickly realize that they were not looking for a relationship, but instead a brief affair, or they'd be put off as soon as they picked up on her quirks.

So, after learning a good many hard lessons in the first ten years of her adulthood, Cora had resolved herself to being alone. She quite liked her own company, though she still enjoyed time with friends and her correspondences. As a young child, she'd always imagined herself with a partner, though she was growing increasingly convinced that it was simply not a viable solution. As such, she'd taken to gently dissuading anyone from setting their cap at her as quickly as she might.

That moment, when Asterion combined those three actions into an equation that finally computed, she was instantly transported back to the first time she'd thought herself in love... and realized it was *so* much worse this time. Not only was he *bound* to be disappointed in her, as that was always the case, but she'd been actively avoiding her own attraction to him for months.

No, it had to be stopped, before he discovered what she was really like and decided she was not worth his time. Luckily, if there was anything she knew, it was what people did *not* like about her and how she could wield them to drive them away. Not one to beat around the bush, Cora resolved to start strong.

Her own fondness for Asterion put her in a uniquely precarious position, so she'd wanted to deal with it as quickly as possible. Instead of treating him coldly or ignoring him, Cora unleashed what she considered to be her secret weapon, shells.

When she was quite young, Cora had spent a great deal of time traveling through the rock of her mountain, melding through it, so as not to disturb its intricate makeup. It was comforting, the entire lack of sound as she was consumed by the steady, comforting pressure and silence. She'd been confused as a child that rock was solid for everyone else all the time. When she willed it, she could move through or mold the rock as if it were air or clay. As she'd explored the interior of her mountain, though, she had encountered curious formations within its strata. According to their best records, the world was less than 10,000 years old, these deposits, called fossils, still dotted the insides of her mountain. To their best guesses, fossils should take thousands and thousands of years to form.[3]

Even though they should not exist, the fossils remained littered throughout her mountain, little nuggets of joy for her to find. Her favorites, she had quickly decided, were those of fossilized sea creatures, and shells. They differed from the present-day shells she could find along her mountain's tiny beach, and she loved imagining a time where her own mountain had been entirely different.

Though she found fossils to be infinitely interesting, their varied textures and colors uniquely adapted to their purpose, she'd learned that sadly, most others did not.

A long, detailed speech covering her favorite topic usually dissuaded even the most determined suitors, a fact she'd been confronted with repeatedly before learning her lesson. And that was fair enough, she figured.

---

3. The timeline the Lady has shared and the geological record are often at odds with each other. Though some posit that instead our Lady operates on a slightly different reckoning of time than mortals, my reading leads me to believe it is more complex. From her journals, we can see how much of the creation of our world was instinctual and based on her observations of other planets. If, for example, she observed fossils from ancient seas in rock on other planets, she'd have included them in her creation of Timonde, though she may not have understood their significance at the time, or ever.

She didn't have much interest or enjoyment in listening to someone blab on, however excitedly, about something she cared nothing about, either. But, in the past, it *had* been a foolproof method of stymying interest. It didn't matter, anymore, if the interest would be welcomed or not, her hobbies were an important part of who she was, and though she could see the appeal of how other nymphs seemed to share affection, people were just too exhausting for Cora to see it as a viable option.

With Asterion, it didn't seem to work the way she'd planned. She'd droned on and on about shells, specifically mollusk reproduction which she assumed he'd find interminably boring, but he'd only nodded. He didn't interrupt her, nor look at her dreamy-eyed as some had done. Instead, he seemed... engaged? Interested? Intrigued? Hell, he'd even asked questions, though not until she'd wound down what she was speaking about, which was even *more* infuriating as she hated being interrupted. Perhaps, she'd hoped, he'd go home and contemplate a lifetime of shell lectures and think better of it.

Instead, he'd brought cookies.

Chapter Two

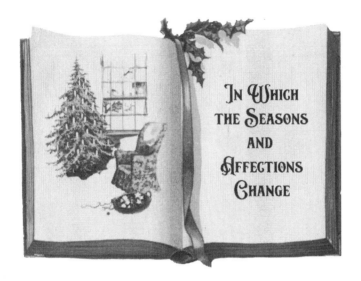

In Which the Seasons and Affections Change

I N THE WEEKS THAT followed the cookie debacle, Cora began to think her methods were working. Asterion still came to the library—as well he should—but he kept his distance and only spoke with her within the confines of her position. His reading still ranged widely, but she found... inconsistencies with his reading habits.

It was possible, of course, the first few times, that he simply picked a book on accident.

When she'd pick up his stacks to re-shelve after he dropped them off, or from his study cubby, they would largely be on a single topic, whichever he was interested in at the time. The outliers though, began to show a suspicious pattern. First, it was a book on various races and their characteristics among his research on the history of the Empire. Next, there was a book on geology amongst a series of culinary works. An anatomy text on nymphs among a grouping of political philosophy texts and finally, the real kicker, shells.

Though he might have been trying to be discreet, when he checked out multiple books on shells for several weeks in a row, Cora knew that she had not actually succeeded. Every one of the extra books had some tangential relation to her, though he'd not tried to engage her in conversation any further. Instead, Asterion was cordial, helpful but not overbearing, and scrupulous in his adherence to the library's rules.

As the seasons changed and the winter solstice neared, his topic of interest shifted once more, with a notable exception. For several weeks, his book choices were entirely uniform. All covered holiday traditions among different cultures, not a shell among them. Perhaps she'd finally lost him? Perhaps she'd misjudged his interest in her and his reading choices had been nothing but a coincidence? Normally, she excelled at spotting patterns, but perhaps her confusing emotions around Asterion interfered with the ability. Regardless, his behavior surely *had* changed of late. He came earlier, stayed later, and took more notes that he had in the past, even falling asleep on more than one occasion. She worried about him actually, but considering how little he engaged with her, she didn't think it would be appropriate.

Why then, didn't she feel relieved? Surely she should rejoice at the reduction in his attention. Shouldn't she be happy that he seemed more intent on study rather than creating conversation with her? At least she should have felt an ease of the fluttering she felt in her stomach when he was around. The man had made her nervous for months, and yet when faced with his waning interest, she felt no triumph. She dragged on for weeks, having difficulty, for the first time, enjoying the holiday season.

She felt no joy at the first touches of snow on her slopes, no comfort in feeling it settle it's calming blanket over her mountain's peak. The chill in the air normally invigorated her, and she'd always loved seeing decorations go up all over the city. She maintained her holiday traditions for the library of course, holding her seasonal story times and highlighting old favorites, but it all felt... hollow.

The bells and holly that so frequently decorated door fronts only annoyed her with their jangling and prickly leaves, and she had trouble mustering the enthusiasm for even wearing her normal ridiculous seasonal wear.

As she sat at her desk, the night before solstice, she slumped in her chair, propping her arms on the tabletop. Outside the library's two-story windows, couples rushed by with last minute purchases or strolled with intricately wrapped packages to visit friends or family. Because it was the first year when there were more than dwarves settled in the city (aside from Cora herself, of course), there were plenty of decorations she didn't recognize, but they all served to evoke a sense of joy and hope... in theory. It *should* have been the most exciting holiday season of her life. Instead, Cora glowered at the wreaths hung in windows and the mistletoe hanging in the doorway of the library.

"Cora! Cora!" A small voice rang out through the stacks. Another voice shushed it and a few seconds later, Broderson and her three children emerged.

"I'm terribly sorry about that," Catrin said, with little Bjorn on her hip.

The first time Cora had seen the woman, she'd honestly thought she was some sort of strange dwarf. She was short, like many dwarfs but had white hair, which only came to dwarves with age. She was human, so Cora had never seen anyone like her. Her three children, however, were all half-orcs, and bore the green skin and size to prove it. Her oldest children, twins, were eight and already they stood eye to eye with their mother.

"Cora," the girl, Ursule, whispered. "I can't wait for you to see our outfits tomorrow!"

Though she tried to be quiet, she did squeal a bit when she spoke.

"Outfits? For what?" It was certainly possible that Catrin might bring the children by on solstice for a visit, but it would certainly spark a new step in their friendship if they spent the holiday together.

"The ball!" Ursule spun in a circle, flaring her skirt out around her legs as her voice took on a dreamy quality.

"Oh," Cora said. "I'm afraid I won't be attending."

"No?" Halsten, Cat's eldest boy piped up.

"I can't, I'm afraid. You see, I've a lot of work to do, and nothing to wear!"

"Oh, that's so sad!" Ursule's face was awash with horror, though Cora couldn't find it in her to sympathize.

A large, stuffy room, packed with people? It sounded a nightmare. Not to mention the fact that Cora would need to make hours of small talk, considering she'd certainly not have anyone to attend with. No, a lack of attire was a perfect excuse to avoid the occasion entirely, and she was grateful to have it.

"Now, kids, let's not pry into Miss Cora's life or reasons for not attending, perhaps you can wear your finery on a special trip to the library some other time!" Catrin said, ushering her children toward the door.

"What a splendid idea! Goodbye dears!" Though she normally loved them, Cora was only too happy to see the family go. The excitement over the ball and all of the other holiday festivities was wearing on her. She'd had more conversations on the matter than she could count, and frankly, she was ready for it all to be finished, and *fast*.

As the hours wore on, Cora finally motivated herself to pack up and head home, such as it was, around ten. She lived on the third floor of the library, with a balcony that overlooked the stacks, but she always made a point to leave through the front doors so she could ensure they were locked up tight. Which, of course, meant confronting the infernal decorations once more. The council was responsible for decorating all public spaces in the city, so she had little say in the outside of the library, which apparently included the doorway. The festive sprig had appeared overnight, and though she herself was a bit of a humbug, she left it previously, not wanting to ruin the tradition for whatever culture it belonged to.

Leaving the library that evening, though, she fetched a ladder to remove it. The mistletoe particularly bothered her, though she was unable to figure out why. Perhaps it was its especially festive nature, with its bright ribbon. Perhaps it was because it marked the entrance of her door, but she didn't understand the significance. Perhaps, it was because she had a sneaking suspicion it was a minotaur tradition.[1]

She hadn't done any research on the matter; she'd not go out of her way to find out such things about Asterion's culture. Instead, she'd just happened to notice, on one of her nightly strolls, that he had one hanging above his lintel, with a similarly shaded ribbon. They were all over, of course, even some dwarves had

---

1. The tradition of mistletoe is indeed a minotaur tradition, among many others..

adopted them, but it didn't *feel* as if it were a simple coincidence.

Removing the mistletoe, like pushing him away, failed to have its desired effect. Instead, she felt like a curmudgeon, stuffing the festive little posy in her pocket before anyone could see. The rest of the decor would be down in a week or so anyhow, and perhaps even if she felt guilty just then, it would do her good to not look at it all day.

Clutching her long winter coat around her, Cora navigated the bustling streets of Berggeheimnis.[2] With her parents away visiting Sanctuary—a city far to the north that housed a group of people who lived free of the Empire's influence—for the holiday, Cora found herself entirely alone. Accompanying them was an impossibility, and Cora didn't begrudge them their important work building connections there. Her holiday the following day, though, would be a quiet, private affair, when she was used to a cozy time with family.

Weaving in between happy faced people, Cora finally arrived at her own door. Built into the side of the cavern wall, she had

---

2. Though the entirety of the city was underground, its cove, open to the ocean, still allowed gusts of wind, bearing the outside climate, to penetrate the mountain and necessitated seasonal attire.

a round door that she and her father had
fitted to a natural opening in the rock. As
she approached her cheery yellow door, Cora
spotted a nondescript package sitting on her
front stoop. Though they were away, her
parents, in their infinite sweetness, must have
arranged for a surprise in their absence.

Picking it up, she noted that the handwriting
on the accompanying card belonged to neither
of her parents, but perhaps their secret
accomplice had labeled it instead. Upon
entering, Cora sat the package and her most
recent novel down on her kitchen table and
stoked the fire. The gift only reminded her
of how alone she was and perhaps she'd
want something to open in the morning. She
changed into some comfortable pajamas and
made herself a modest meal of cold roast beef,
mustard, hard cheese and bread. She brewed a
cup of tea, and huddled up, as she was wont to
do of an evening, with her supper and her book
near the fire.

As she ate, with a book purchased with her
own money lest she smudge it, the words swam
in front of her eyes, the blurriness of tears
marring her vision. She hadn't any idea why she
was crying. She *liked* to keep her own company.
Her chest gave a shot of pain that countered
her insistence. She was *very* lonely, after all.

She'd dreamt of a home filled with warmth and laughter, of children she could adore, who would bear only half of her abilities and be able to explore the world in ways she couldn't. She'd dreamt of a life that expanded her own world enough that she didn't care it was confined to a singular mountain. But the walls of her cozy home felt as if they closed in on her, limiting the extent of her life with their constriction.

Tears fell heavy, marring the pages of her book. Her food tasted bland, her increasingly stuffy nose dampening the taste.

It was no use, her food tasted like nothing, and she wasn't hungry anyhow. Cora stood to return her plate to the table and fetch a handkerchief. The small package waited there for her, a small point of brightness in an increasingly dark day. Perhaps she needed the joy it would bring tonight more than in the morning. Admiring the simple but tidy wrapping, she pulled the card off the rich red paper.

Chapter Three

In Which the Written Word is More Powerful than Cora Ever Imagined

*D*EAR CORA,

    I fear I may have misstepped, adhering to customs which you do not follow, and inadvertently hurt you, or our chances. Still, I'm a man who knows his own heart, and it is set on you. When a minotaur decides to court someone, we take it upon ourselves to study our hopeful partners. During that time, we are not wont to socialize with them, as we might be tempted to ask them for information instead of work for it. I have tried my best to study all that pertains to you and learned early on in my research about the mating habits of nymphs. I immediately felt as if such habits did not fit what I knew of you and set to court you in the minotaur fashion instead. I can only hope this was not entirely in error.

You see, the end of this study culminates in a grand gesture which should prove to our hopeful mate how we value them. Over the course of this eve, I will deliver to you three gifts, representing the past, the present, and the future I hope to share. Expect the first gift when the bell tolls one.

Ever yours,

Asterion

Cora's hands shook, the letter rattling in her grip. Asterion had *not* abandoned her? In fact, he'd spent weeks, perhaps months, building to whatever he was to do that very night? She could scarcely believe her eyes, but her curiosity could stand it no longer and she ripped at the red paper. Was this the first gift, come early? Or would there be an additional gift? If so, what could this small package hold?

A small box waited inside, and she lifted the lid to reveal... cookies. They were small, a pale brown that darkened at the edges and shaped like seashells. Nestled between them was another sprig of mistletoe, that same festive ribbon tied in a neat bow. Attached was another note.

You wouldn't let me give you my gift of cookies, though it symbolized my intention of courting you seriously. These are called Madeleines. I know not why, but they are delectable little treats (one of my favorite things in the world) shaped like shells (one of your favorite things). I wanted to hang this bundle of mistletoe over your door but feared to do so without you knowing it's significance. In Cretia, where I am from, we hang such things from doorframes, and everyone must kiss if they meet at that threshold. Hanging one in your doorframe, you see, would be presumptuous. Expect the first gift when the bell tolls one.

-A

The delicate cookies were artfully arranged, and Cora almost left them as they were. But, she supposed, if Asterion had gone to the trouble of making them, he'd surely intended for her to eat them. Extracting one dainty shell, she lifted it to her mouth, biting into the crispy exterior. Inside, it was smooth and light, buttery with a hint of almond and ever so gently sweetened. Though she had never had one before, the taste and texture instantly transported her to her childhood, of lazing away the hours on a mountainside meadow, picking out shapes in the clouds, or watching for dragons as they flew in and out of their caldera. The sweet tang of nostalgia echoed through her with each bite so strongly she could almost smell the warm grass.

With gentle fingers, she extracted the mistletoe, twirling it in her fingers as she thought. If Asterion had done that much work... she could at least appreciate his efforts. Her feelings on the matter, and him especially, were all a jumble as she scurried to her bedroom. It was getting late, and if she had three surprises coming, she'd probably appreciate being a *little* rested.

After changing into her nightgown, she snuggled into her bed, the light of her candle flickering against the wall. She knew, should she want, she could simply turn on her gas lamps, but there was something so magical about candlelight that she enjoyed, and it seemed like a night for magic. Her nerves were jangling about, though she tried to remind herself that it might be nothing but a prank. A cruel one at that.

Still, she could hardly contain her excitement as she took a draught to help her sleep and pulled the curtains of her bed closed.

"**B**ONG!" THE CLANGING OF the grandfather clock woke Cora from sleep. In truth, she'd roused each time it sounded, though some magic of the night had allowed her to drift off easily, regardless. As the clock sounded one, though, she burst from her bed, eyes flying open as she rushed down the hall to her front door.[1]

The sound of singing, dulled by her door, nudged just at the edge of her hearing. It seemed... quiet and when she opened the door, she saw why. A group of carolers, dressed up in holiday finery surrounded Asterion. He looked quite fine himself, with the drapey clothing of his people festooned with holly at the brooch, and a circlet of mistletoe on his head. Each of the carolers held candles and whispered as much as sang her favorite carol.

In front of him, Asterion held a large sign, or rather, a series of them, as she quickly realized.

"*Cora,*" said the first. He dropped it, and the second revealed still more words. "*Your first gift represents the past. I hope, over time we will learn each other's...*"

He revealed the third sign. "*But until we do...*"

---

1. I don't often poke fun at my subjects, but it just strikes me that one does not "rush" down the hallway to someone they feel decidedly lukewarm about.

"I hope you'll settle for a few fossils."

Cora pressed her hand against her mouth. She'd expected *gifts*, but already this was the most elaborate thing anyone had ever done for her. Tears spilled over onto her cheeks, but she couldn't stop smiling.

"You've been such a help to me..."

"And I've been enamored with you since the day I met you..."

"When you told me about your love of shells..."

"I knew you were the one."

"I know I'm not as smart..."

"Or as kind..."

"Or as patient..."

"Or as beautiful as you..."

"But I hope you'll consider giving me a chance."

"Just like you've taught me that shells have worn away..."

"And been replaced with other mineral deposits..."

"(See, I listen!)"

Cora giggled through her hand, overwhelmed. Apparently he *did* listen.

"I'd love to learn more about your *past."*

The carolers wrapped up their song, with Asterion holding the last note, his surprisingly beautiful voice warming her from the inside out.

Holding out a box, Asterion stepped forward. "If um, if it's alright that I return at two, please hang the mistletoe outside your door."

Cora sniffled and nodded her head, too choked up to reply, but his eyes lit up at her nod anyhow.

The carolers milled about awkwardly. Perhaps they were waiting for some bigger display, but if she was honest, this amount of fanfare was just about perfect.

Asterion beamed, shuffling his feet before slowly turning away, his eyes staying locked to hers until he was facing nearly entirely away from her. Seconds later, he turned back, waving with his full arm over his head. Then, the cheeky man lowered his hand and *blew her a kiss!*

The white marble hue of her skin had never hidden the pink of a blush very well, and now it was on full display. Hardly able to contain herself, she slapped her hand to her mouth and blew one back. What had come over her? Was it the holiday? The magic of the night? Asterion? Or was it simply the feeling of being truly seen for the first time in years?

Once he was out of sight, Cora scurried back inside to open her gift. Inside, carefully nestled among packing paper, was an arresting assortment of fossils. First, she picked up an

opalized Trigonia, the light from her
entryway reflecting off its varied colors
and painting her walls. Next came a
beautifully preserved iridescent Ammonite,
and a Gastropoda that she'd need to look
up for more information. A small but–if
she made her guess correctly–exceedingly
rare snail shell was the last item before
she encountered another layer of paper. She
peeled it away, because the box still felt
heavy, and her breath caught at what was
within.

Filling the bottom of the box, its frills
preserved in pristine detail, was a blue coral.
She'd been named for coral, as she'd formed
near a section of fossilized coral. With a thrill
of excitement, she brought the blue coral
into her room and set it on her bureau. She
smiled at how lovely it looked paired with her
opalized version.

It was only one fifteen by the clock at
her bedside, which meant three quarters of
an hour to stew in her feelings and debate
hanging the mistletoe.

So far at least, none of it seemed like an
elaborate prank. And anyhow, Asterion had
never struck her as one to be so cruel. As she
climbed back into bed, her curtains open so
she could admire her new shells. She twirled

the sprig, images of what it might be like to be loved by Asterion dancing in her head.

Chapter Four

IN WHICH A
PHAETON
ISN'T A SLEIGH
BUT IS
ROMANTIC
NONETHELESS

F IVE MINUTES BEFORE THE hour, Cora was
pacing between the door into the library
and her front door, unable to sleep. Her nerves
were wound so tight that she nearly jumped out
of her skin when the great grandfather clock
began chiming two. The last vestiges of the
bell faded from the air were quickly followed
by a few swift raps on her front door. Hands
shaking, she opened it to find only Asterion this
time, waiting with a bouquet of flowers.

"You hung the mistletoe," he said, his voice filled with awe. "I wasn't sure you would."

"If you've gone to all this trouble, I might as well give you the opportunity to see, firsthand, if you're truly interested."

"I am," he said. Asterion held out the flowers to her, thrusting them so she had to grab them swiftly, lest they drop on the ground. They weren't fancy, just simple camellias, though they happened to be her favorite flower. Asterion held out his hand for hers, and Cora brushed her golden braid, and considered that she was in her nightdress.

"I've a blanket and cloak in the phaeton," he reassured.

The only way she'd find out the plan for this gift seemed to be following him, so she placed her hand in his, as gentle as a bird alighting on a branch.

His palm dwarfed hers, he could engulf her entire hand fully in his should he want.

"Where are we off to then?" she asked.

"It's a surprise!" Asterion said. His eyes were bright, and he squeezed her hands as he led her down the terraces to where a phaeton waited with a matched pair of horses at the helm. It was an odd sort of phaeton, it seemed they would stand, as there were no seats. Asterion helped her inside and wrapped a thick, burgundy cloak around her shoulders. Draped over the edge of the phaeton was a matching garment, presumably for Asterion.

"It's not quite a sleigh, but I know how to drive this." Asterion sounded hesitant, looking at her as if asking for forgiveness. "There's also a distinct lack of snow."

"This is lovely! Why would you want a sleigh over this?"

"The song, the one you've been humming for the last few weeks, it mentions a sleigh ride in the snow? It seemed like it might be your favorite."

"It is." Had he really paid such close attention? It seemed he had, if he'd noticed her humming, a habit she rarely even realized she was doing. "Are you–" Asterion clicked his tongue and the pair of horses lurched forward.

The motion put Cora off her balance, though Asterion's large hand steadied her on her waist. He removed it nearly as fast as he'd placed it, but the heat of where he touched her lingered, spreading throughout her body. For months, she'd denied attraction to him, afraid to let herself explore her feelings for the friendly, if needy, minotaur.

"It seems you've been paying attention," she noted. "My favorite flowers and the song..."

"You could say so," Asterion said, leading them through the great city of Berggeheimnis.

Cora's unique living situation in the library meant that she lived in a largely municipal section of the city. As such, their drive took them through some of the most elaborate buildings, each one an edifice of dwarven architecture. It was normal for wreaths to decorate the city, but as she paid attention, Cora picked out other decor that she didn't recognize.

"Are any of these decorations from your home?"

"The mistletoe, as well as the boats, but there's an array, really. I tried to represent as many cultures as I could."

"You tried? Did you do all this?" she asked.

"Oh no, no!" Asterion chuckled. "I couldn't possibly, I had a team to help me. I just told them where to put things."

"But you picked it all out? Designed it all?" It was a massive feat, Berggeheimnis was said to be the second biggest city in the world after Pentweagh. "Is that what all of those books were about? The ones on holidays?"

Asterion smiled wide, though he only took his eyes off the road for a brief second. "Exactly! I didn't know much about all of these new cultures, let alone how they celebrate during Yule, so I had to do research."

"Well, you certainly seemed to do a lot. What did you find?"

"There's a lot of variation, to be sure, but there's a lot of similarity too. Celebrations from across the continent will at times have shockingly similar traditions."

"Really?" Cora asked, her interest truly piqued. "That's fascinating!"

"I thought so! For example, for reasons I can't quite understand, we minotaurs seem to share a great deal of traditions with cyclopes and strangely, a few types of sea monsters. Whereas you and the dwarves here in Berggeheimnis actually share more with several colonies of werewolves."

Asterion's chest was puffed out now, as if her interest had inflated him. At first, he hadn't struck her as being particularly bright, and frankly he'd seemed entirely unprepared for... well the entirety of his task in the city.

"I'd never have thought that!"

They wound through the streets of the city, the glow of crystal street lamps had been dimmed hours before, but over the past few weeks, the eternally mesmerizing city of Berggeheimnis transformed into a riotous celebration of winter even without the citizens.

As an oread, Cora was tied to the mountain, ever aware of it around her.[1] The silence of the sleeping city let her connect even closer, in ways she'd normally have to delve deeper into its stone to do. Without the hustle of daily life shifting around, the mountain pulsed through her, its contentment with itself a steady beat that matched the heart in her chest.

Within the confines of the library, she never had trouble dealing with groups of people. The library was structured, her interactions largely followed a similar set of scripts, the rules definite and easy to enforce. Outside though? Things were often...unpredictable. Crowd and noise levels varied, at times in unpredictable ways, and Cora found she needed to be in the right frame of mind for such excursions.

Asterion didn't press the conversation, letting her enjoy the ride through the city.

They left the main cavern and turned off into a side cavern "We're leaving the city?" Cora asked, her voice tight. "I can't leave the mountain."

"We won't, I did my research." Asterion's voice was low and rumbly, it reminded her of the voice of the mountain she heard sometimes.

---

1. Oread is the specific name for a nymph who is bound to a mountain, as opposed to a tree like a dryad.

Less of an actual sound, but more of a feeling that she innately understood.

"You did, didn't you? You seem to do a lot of that..."

Asterion chuckled, rubbing his horn in a way she'd seen him do frequently when reading. "I have to. I'm interested in learning, but we minotaurs aren't exactly known for being scholars."

He blushed and Cora thought it was one of the most adorable things she'd ever seen. Not to mention that while they'd spoken a great deal in the library, it had almost entirely consisted of him inquiring about books on different subjects–save her verbal dissertation on shells which she'd subjected him to.

"So, it's something you were excited to be able to do, when you arrived? Study?" Cora perked up at the notion. She loved learning and was always chagrined at how few people seemed inclined to agree. Those that did congregated in her library, of course, but for so many, it was a chore.

"Not at all, at first, I had to. I haven't had much book learning' ye see and needed to catch up. I'm not stupid, mind, it's just not something we ever needed to do, really. Needing that sort of education was something that we didn't

foresee, so my parents raised me the best
they knew."

Cora tried to keep the disappointment
from her face when he mentioned necessity.

"But now," he blew air between his lips. " It's
like I'm thirsty and can't get enough water.
There's just so much I don't know? How am
I supposed to get to all of it? I think I could
live my whole life and not even read all of the
books in your library."

Now *that* was what she'd been hoping to
hear! It truly didn't matter if Asterion had
always loved learning, that he did so now was
more than enough to give her hope that he
might not find her so... odd.

"If you didn't do much schooling, what did
you spend your time on?" she asked.

"Practical things, carpentry, gardening,
practical engineering, that sort of thing."

"Oh?" Cora knew little of practical
application, aside from how one should
organize a library. Certainly nothing on the
subjects or gardening or carpentry.

"We're a bit mad for traps and mazes back
home. So many of our exports are security
measures, many of which are sold to the
Empire. Everyone on the council tries to
pretend that they value our input, but really,

they mostly care about our defenses. Especially those we sell to the Empire."

Cora scrunched her nose. "That can't feel good."

"No, and I didn't help my case much when I showed up, still wet behind the ears. I'm out of my depth, but I'll make them respect me, yet." He set his jaw in a way that made Cora believe he'd do it. But why would he say such a thing to her, wasn't the point of the whole evening to impress her? To convince her that he'd be a worthy mate? It seemed counterintuitive to show such vulnerability.

"What is this all about then, this evening? Shouldn't you be trying to impress me? isn't that how this works?"

"Honestly, I'm not sure. There wasn't much in the books on nymph mating habits, and even though I figured you might be used to the dwarven way, I'm no good at boasting, so I'm just going about it the minotaur way. Well, at least partially anyhow. I haven't had much opportunity to show off my physical prowess, so that bit is out. The rest of it though, is really just me showing you—as best I can, who I am. As much as I want to be with you... I don't want you going into it with any false notions about who I am. My actions will have to say what I can't, because I'm no good at it."

They were well within the depths of the mountain now, the crystal lanterns swinging from the horses' harness. If he was trying to make her feel safe, Asterion was going about it the right way, to be sure. The familiar walls of her mountain around her, and a warm cloak around her shoulders were a balm to her usual anxiety.

Cora could feel them nearing the edge of the mountain, like a coat rapidly thinning and exposing her to the cold. Asterion pulled the phaeton over to the side of the passageway. Asterion leapt from the phaeton and held out his hands before him.

"Stay right here, I need to check on a few last-minute things, I will be right back!"

The clops of his hooves on the stone floor gave way to the crunch of snow beneath him. If she'd wanted to, Cora could have gotten a sense as to what he was doing via her connection to the mountain, but wanted it to be a surprise. She could hear him walking around, and every so often he would make another noise that she couldn't quite place.

While she waited, Cora fingered the smooth abalone shell she kept in her pocket in attempts to keep the anxiety at bay. The repetitive motion grounded her, but not nearly as much as it usually did.

"All right, I'm ready! " Asterion's voice traveled to her from outside.

The phaeton was higher than Cora realized without Asterion to lift her down, so she was glad that he wasn't present to see her disgraceful exit. As always happened, she felt herself leave the interior of the mountain like she was passing through a thin veil of fabric. The pool of her magic, and its connection to the mountain, still tied her through her feet, but otherwise, she lost some of that sense of connection. The sight before her though, wiped any thought of her connection from her mind.

Amid a sea of lights in the night sky, Asterion stood before a veritable feast. He had brought her to an outcropping overlooking the ocean, the stars reached him, and reflected on the water. Around him, candles littered the outcropping. On the ground, what looked to be several layers of thick furs were festooned with all matter of food. Many had closures over top, though Cora could see a selection of meats and cheeses, fruits, and pastries.

And in the middle, was the best sight of all, Asterion. His chest was heaving, his cheeks ruddy in the night air. His breaths puffed out of him, the only clouds in the sky. He was a vision of virility and light, putting all others to shame.

His mouth stretched wide in a smile, and his ears perked up.

He looked at the picture of confidence, a powerful God, who saw fit to grace the night with his presence.

"It's my understanding that most people here share a feast with their family the night before Yule. Since neither of us have family here this year, I hoped that, even for just this one hour, you'd consider being mine."

His mention of the meal, and her lack of family made her throat sting. Normally, she *would* have had dinner with her family, and as much as she told herself she was fine with being lonely, the pain she felt said otherwise. She couldn't find her voice, so she simply smiled and nodded. Asterion waved one massive hand over a section of furs, indicating she should sit. When she sat, he settled across from her and pulled two plates from a basket. Next, he retrieved two wooden flagons, and filled them with steaming mulled wine. Despite his outward confidence, Asterion seemed to have trouble meeting her eyes, and his hands shook when he handed her things.

Though she denied her attraction to him for months, she knew her frequent annoyance with him was largely caused by frustration. It was one thing to know that nearly everyone expected her to be different than she was, to acknowledge that should anyone come to truly know her, they would likely be disappointed. It was another thing entirely to be confronted by someone she could truly admire with that knowledge. To face the fact that they too, might expect her to be someone else, someone that would conform to what they wanted of her.

But to be his? Perhaps she might be able to risk it. He'd at least shown that he'd listened to her when she spoke of her interests, and that had to count for something, didn't it? That he'd asked for it, that he wanted that with her, stole her breath.

"I think that sounds lovely, actually."

Asterion smiled again, and Cora was confronted with a strange new reality, one where she'd risk everything once more to see that smile on his face.

When Asterion smiled, his entire being smiled. His cheeks lifted and his nose pulled and scrunched. His eyebrows raised, as if he could not possibly believe what was happening. But his smile didn't stop there, his shoulders raised and his hands cupped, he shifted forward on his hooves, and behind him, she could see his tail swaying back and forth.

That smile? That was a whole-body smile that you could live to see. It was a smile that could get you out of bed, or–she considered with a smile of her own–a smile that could get you into it.

He didn't meet her eyes as much as she expected. It was something she'd learned over the years that people did, and she'd adopted it, and so many other mannerisms, so she especially noticed when someone failed to do them, and always wondered at why. This time, she also noted that his cheeks were red, and perhaps not from just the cold. Was he embarrassed? Shy?

How much did she know about Asterion before he delivered madeleines to her door? She knew *some*, of course. She knew about the way he stuck his tongue out to the side when he read, she knew how he always tried to manage a pile of books that was clearly too tall. She knew that he had trouble containing his excitement when he found an interesting fact... but so much else of what she knew, she realized, had come from their brief conversation earlier.

In one short night, she'd learned more about him, Asterion, not the diplomat, but the man himself, than she'd ever known about many people.

"So," she started. "How are you finding Berggeheimnis?"

Asterion tilted his head to the side, considering. "It's larger than I expected... when you hear of a city inside a cave, I suppose you expect connected caverns, like a labyrinth, but dark. I about lost my nerve when I realized how open it all was. Minotaurs, you see, we like close spaces. We don't mind what's above us, ceiling or sky, like, but we like good solid walls around. When we sailed into the harbor, everything felt so...wide. Like I said, I almost turned to the captain and told him to take me home right then." He piled a plate full of small bites and traded her for her empty one. "It's one reason I like the library so much. The bookshelves divide it up, and even if you have those big windows looking out over the city, you know you're enclosed... protected."

Cora nodded; she knew the feeling. "Like somehow the separation, the glass, makes seeing it all a bit easier..."

"Exactly! My house, well, it's very lovely, but I don't know how much they knew about minotaurs when they picked it for me. It's uh, very *open*." He scrunched his nose up, and his tail gave a sharp twitch to the side. "I bought some dividers, so I could sleep, but the place doesn't have any walls... at all. It's just a large cave, really."

"I know exactly what you mean, I felt it when they created it. I think they assumed that would be what you'd prefer. Really, it must be horrid for you!"

"Don't think of it, I know it was an attempt to make me feel welcome. It just happens that it was exactly wrong.[2] It's why I come to the library so often. Hell, the day of my first council meeting, I left and dreaded going home. I stood outside the chambers for probably ten minutes trying to work up the courage. Then, I remembered my tour, and how I'd felt in the library. So, I decided I needed to do some reading."

"I remember that day... you wandered in like a lost puppy!" Cora giggled and popped a grape in her mouth.

"I was! Lost and alone, with no idea what I was doing and then... there you were." He met her eyes then, so serious and vulnerable that it made Cora's heart ache as much as her stomach flutter. "You helped me... I know you were just doing your job, but I'll always be grateful for that day. I don't even care if you were so nice

---

2. A few days later, Cora looked into what was documented and she was enraged to find that if they had done even rudimentary research on his culture, instead of assuming minotaurs would want open spaces like cattle, they'd have known that minotaurs prefer mazes for living.

because you felt bad for me, because you gave me things I didn't even know I needed. I'd only just started to realize how much I didn't know about where I was and what I was supposed to be doing, but you gave me the tools to keep on with it and eventually, to do as well as I like to think I have."

"Whatever you've accomplished, you've earned yourself," Cora said, placing her hand on his and squeezing. "I showed you resources, sure, but you've put in so much hard work, it's honestly inspiring."

She'd touched his hand impulsively, because she needed to reassure him, and to stop him from dismissing all he'd done, but she couldn't bring herself to remove it. In the cold air, his large hands dwarfed her own. He had thick, blunt fingers that ended in squared off nails. He was lightly furred there, she realized, like a peach. Her breath caught, looking at the juxtaposition. Her own pale skin, devoid of color save the veins of gold running through her was a shock against his. And the heat. He was so *hot*, pulsing heat through her hand, melting through her like a river of honey.

After several moments of awed silence, Asterion cleared his throat. "Either way, coming to the library that day was probably the best choice I've ever made."

Chapter Five

IN WHICH TIME IS LOST, A HOMECOMING, AND MINOTAUR MATING CUSTOMS ARE OBSERVED

T HEY ATE AND TALKED, the conversation flowed easily–shockingly so. Asterion didn't seem to mind when Cora spoke at length, and he was an attentive listener, nodding his head and asking insightful questions about her childhood, the city, and of course, shells.

When it was time to pack up the food, Cora could scarcely believe how quickly the time had passed.

"Is it an hour already?" she asked when Asterion began tidying.

"Past time, honestly, I am probably a bit late on gift number three at this point, so I hope you'll forgive the tardiness. It was just so nice I didn't... didn't want to leave and break the spell." He smiled, sadly, lifting only one side of his mouth. "I asked you for an hour, and I am afraid I took more than that."

"I said I'd try, for an hour, but it was up to me, after that, wasn't it?"

His ears fluttered. "Aye."

Curse him, those ears were adorable, she could see them quickly becoming a weakness.

"Then..." She drew in a fortifying breath. "I think I'd like to keep trying."

"Truly?" Asterion's face lit up. He sped up his cleaning, tidying things up, but not entirely, it was more like he was stowing things rather than cleaning it all up. Was he just going to leave a mess like this? Right on the side of her mountain?

"Shouldn't we take that with us?" She asked.

"I have a friend who will be by in a little bit to clean it up, don't worry."[1]

---

1. If she'd dug, she'd find that the friend he had to help cleanup was the partner of her own friend, Catrin.

He had a plan then, she liked that. Plans were tidy. Of course, one couldn't always count on their plan and its perfect execution, but somehow having one had always made her feel better. When things were sufficiently stowed, if not cleaned up, Asterion held out his hand for hers once more. His hands were cooler now, though still warm, their wide expanse engulfing hers easily. "So smooth," he murmured. Drawing his thumb across the back of her hand. "Your skin, I suppose I expected it to feel cold, or maybe bumpy, somehow?"

"I'm warm-blooded, though you can probably see that my skin is much more like polished marble that's flexible. Other oreads or earth nymphs might have textured skin, I don't really know. Our nature means that some of us tend to be isolated. I've always been a little jealous of dryads, living in the forest together. I don't even know if my neighboring mountains have nymphs, though I can see the dryads dancing in the forest sometimes." She smiled sadly and shrugged.

Asterion led her into the cave and helped her back into the phaeton.

"And your parents? Were they nymphs as well?"

"No," she chuckled. "My parents are dwarfs. It's not uncommon for nymphs to be born of want. So, more often than not, we are born of desire for a child, rather than physical desire. In my case, there was definitely no physical desire involved." Asterion frowned down at her, confused. She didn't cry, thinking of her parent's difficult marriage, but she could see the question in his eyes.

"My mother hasn't said it straight out, but I'm fairly certain that I was some last-ditch attempt to save my parents' marriage. It didn't work, but they tried, for a few years at least."

Saying it out loud brought to mind all the reasons she hadn't ever allowed herself to hope for love. Because, after all, if her mother and father who were two of the best people she knew, couldn't make their love last, how could anyone hope to do so? They still spent a great deal of time together, being that they worked together, but it seemed their love had never been enough.

"That sounds... uncomfortable to know." Asterion squeezed her hand as he mounted the phaeton and took up the reins. "But I imagine it's also some sort of small consolation. To know how badly your mother wanted you?"

"It is, and in truth, my father wanted a child quite badly as well. It was honestly part of what kept them together for as long as they were. At night, they would sit by the fire, and speak about what their baby might be like... those conversations lead to my creation."

"Let me guess, their home was made out of white marble?" he asked with a smirk.

"You *did* do your research. One day, my father, who is quite the craftsman, swore he could begin to see the outline of a baby in the stone. He took out his stone-cutting tools and over the course of a week, freed me from the rock."

"I suppose you could say that your father liberated you, rather than your mother."

"Yes, but she was involved, of course. In fact, when my father freed me from the rock, I was not yet alive. It wasn't until my mother held me and cried that I took my first breath. Neither of them expected me to be alive, but my mother says that when my father pulled me out, I was just so perfect, everything they had ever wished for, that it broke her heart, knowing she would never actually have it. When she cradled me, the desperation she felt held enough magic to bring me to life. Well that, and all that my father poured into the rock as he carved me out."[2]

---

2. As best I can tell, all nymphs are created in response to a great want, and then the magic inherent in the continent of Caihalaith fulfills the need by coalescing to create life.

"I read about how nymphs are formed, but you were a bit of a puzzle to me. I admit, I had more reading planned."

"You've been busy lately, your reading habits have changed, too."

Asterion blushed, his ears wiggling. "Yes, I uh−needed to focus my research ahead of the holidays."

"Oh?"

"They put me in charge of the holiday festivities. As far as I could tell, it's a bit of a trial, to see if I can do it. It was really important to me that I not mess it up, since it's my opportunity to show them that I am not an idiot."

"Of course you aren't!" Cora could hardly believe such a thing! "I don't see any of them in my library day and night with their noses in books!"

Cora was so annoyed that it took her a moment to realize what he meant by being in charge of the festivities.

"Wait a moment, does that mean you are in charge of the decorations?"

He nodded.

"And the holiday market?"

Another nod.

"The ball and the−Asterion! That is so much work!"

"It hasn't been easy, I'll tell you that! It's part of why I wanted to plan tonight for you. I've needed every spare moment to get everything ready for the town, I worried that you'd think I forgot you..."

Cora smiled and looked away, though the second she did, she realized they were in a quite close cave, and she looked like an idiot being suddenly interested in a wall, when really it was obvious she was just being shy. "It likely worked to your advantage... I sort of thought you had, and then I realized that maybe I was disappointed about that... This was certainly a surprise."

"Do you think you can forgive me then, for my lack of attention the last several weeks? I wanted to make sure that I wasn't messing it up again, like I did with the cookies. I am sorry for that, by the way. Back then, I didn't know where you lived, and following you to find out, or ambushing you when you left for the night both seemed..."

"Creepy?"

"Let's say uncouth."

"Oho! Whipping out the big words, are you?"

"I've got to! The girl I'm interested in, you see, she's more into big words than big–ahem–sorry, *that* was also uncouth."

Cora giggled and covered her face. "No, no, it was funny! Do you normally woo women with big *other* things?" She bumped his shoulder, inviting him to tease back.

Asterion coughed, rubbing a horn. "Well, it's not as if I lead with it—"

"Unless of course, you're *very* happy? Then you might have no choice but to *lead* with it!"

"You little minx!" Asterion looked down at her in shock.

"Sorry," Cora gasped. "I like teasing, and word play, and just playing in general."

"No, I like it," he said softly. "I think I'll like playing with you."

"Oh, point scored! But I did set you up for that one."

"You did, I'm just glad I didn't miss it. I'll have to brush up on my wordplay."

"But really..." Cora looked down at Asterion's clothing. It was drape-y and he didn't seem to wear trousers with it, as his furred legs stuck out the bottom of his tunic. "Is that something you have trouble with... leading when you don't mean to? It doesn't seem like your chiton would do you any favors there."

Eyes blinking, Asterion was silent for a moment. "Well, no, I'm a gentleman, I tie it to my leg, of course."

"You what?" It was Cora's turn to blink now.

"Well, I certainly can't have it flopping about, or God's help me, *leading* anywhere!"

"Well, now I am just curious!" The words flew out of her mouth before she could stop them, and she realized that they were true... In more ways than one. Asterion intrigued her in a way that no one had in a long, long time.

She might have learned to be wary of people looking to her for casual sex, but that didn't mean she wasn't interested.[3]

And where Asterion was concerned, she was very interested. She bit her lip, her core heating at the thought.

"Well, I certainly won't object to you being curious, I just—well, I sort of assumed it might not be something you were interested in at all..."

"Oh?"

"At first, I wondered if you just didn't realize I was interested, if cultural differences were getting in the way. Then, after you seemed to understand, I messed up with the cookies, and then, well I backed off in hopes that you'd show me, if you were, I mean..."

---

3. Cora's situation and Asterion's involvement on the council has led to a concerted effort to help different races overcome the stereotypes about them that have been spread by the Empire. While some are partially true, like this of nymphs, they are almost universally harmful, regardless.

"Asterion, I–I am afraid I am not very good at this sort of thing, so I'll just be honest. I haven't had good luck in this area. Others haven't been keen after really knowing me. From what I can tell, I am a relatively good time in bed, but I also realized, over time, that was all some people wanted me for. And if I am going to be involved with someone... I want more than that. I was trying to drive you away when I talked to you about mollusk reproduction, because that is who I am, and I couldn't bear liking you more than I already did if you were only going to leave when you saw the side of me people tend not to like."

Asterion's eyes were half-lidded and tender when he looked down at her, his warm hand coming up to cup her cheek. "So, what I am hearing is, you like me." He smiled and rubbed his thumb over her cheek. "I hate to tell you, it had the exact opposite effect. It solidified, for me, how much I wanted you. It meant a lot to me that you wanted to share what you liked, that you thought I was smart enough to understand."

"I did, I do–I mean I thought to use it to drive you away, of course, but only because people tend to find it incredibly boring... not because you wouldn't understand it."

"If someone else was talking about it, I probably would have found it boring, but you just got so excited that it was hard to not be interested. I suppose I also knew you liked fossils already because you have them everywhere, so that made it easier to know it mattered. Plus," his ears wiggled, and Cora thought he might do that when blushing. "Your nose does this adorable wrinkly thing when you get excited, so even if I got bored, I could always look at that."

Cora couldn't stop smiling for the entire drive home. When they pulled up to her door, there was a tension in her chest, at knowing Asterion might be leaving.

"What now? It's certainly past three..."

Three in the morning and here she was, asking to stay up later? What had come over her?

Then again, it wasn't as if the library were open in the morning, nor was she expected anywhere... she had no reason to wake early. The night had a magic to it that might fade in the light of day. What if she woke to find it nothing but a dream? No, she needed to savor the night, lest it all melt in the light of day.

"It is, which means it is time for your next gift," Asterion reached into his cloak and extracted a small box.

Cora's breath hitched. The entire night had been special, magical even, but somehow, jewelry seemed like a massive step that she wasn't certain she was ready for. Jewelry meant commitment. It meant claiming herself, publicly, for someone else. Her vision focused on the small velvet box. On how Asterion's hands dwarfed it. How he could hide it away from everyone by curling his fingers. Asterion's hands shook as he held it out to her.

That shake, the trembling of his strong hands is what did her in. It's what convinced her that she should at least entertain the idea of looking at what he presented. Looking didn't mean accepting, didn't mean commitment. It meant...exploring. Entertaining the idea of moving forward in a real, tangible way. In a way that might allow her to get hurt, true, but also a way that could allow her intimacy in ways she had never known.

She'd shown Asterion the parts of her others had rejected, practically shoved them in his face.

And yet, there he stood, holding a small box with hands that shook so hard she feared he might drop it. Maybe he was as nervous as she was? Maybe the chance...might be worth it?

With her own unsteady hand, Cora bridged the distance between them, the milliseconds slowing so much that she noticed the dim purple glow of the street-crystals, the cheery dim orange of the crystals dotting the library. Meeting Asterion's eyes, so openly vulnerable, unlocked a part of her she hadn't even known existed. A part that though she ignored, she'd also actively hid her entire life.

Vulnerability, after all, opened one to hurt. But, somehow, it also invited connection. Her hand rasped against the smooth leather box, and with a deep breath, she allowed herself to open it.

Inside, reflecting the light of the crystals, was a beautiful, smooth ring, with a bead of white marble in the center. The odd thing though, was how massive it was. "Asterion, this is beautiful but, I think it's–"

"A little large?"

"Well, yes."

He chuckled, removing the ring from the box. "It's not for you, long term at least." He held the ring up, in front of his face, under his nose. "It's a minotaur thing. I knew I should have given you the book first, but then I would have to stand here while you read it, and that felt stupid and–"

"Asterion, just tell me about it." She placed a hand on his arm and was shocked at how warm he felt. His skin was lightly furred, even where it looked like he wasn't, like a peach.

"Oh, quite. Well... this is sort of like a wedding ring, I suppose, but minotaurs wear them in our noses. Don't worry though it's not... I am not asking you to get married... right now at least. When we are seriously interested in someone, in pursuing something seriously, in a way we hope could end in marriage, a minotaur will gift their partner their ring. You're supposed to ensure it's specific to the person. This one is marble and gold like your skin, I had made especially for you. And then this–" He moved, and now that he pointed it out, Cora could see that there was a delicate gold chain dangling from it. "This allows you to keep it, until you decide that you do want to mate–er, marry. We can mate before then... I mean, if we mate..."

Asterion's face was bright red, his ears wiggling adorably as he fumbled his words.

"I see, so one partner gives this to the other to indicate... serious intent? Perhaps like a courtship?"

"Yes!" Asterion seemed so relieved, though his shout was a *bit* jarring. "And it goes around your waist, so you don't need to show it if you don't want to. In fact, most people wear it next to their skin. If you decide that you'd like to marry, then you'd give it back to me, ideally by piercing me yourself, but I understand if that is a bit much when you weren't raised expecting that you might do that."

"Should I have something for you?" Cora was intrigued by the idea but felt immediately unsure about if it was something she should reciprocate.

"Normally, if you were a minotaur, yes, though both things sort of... move on their own time frame? Like, you aren't expected to have one ready for me, you'd give it to me when you felt ready to commit to me. It's a statement of your own investment to the relationship. In some cases, it doesn't even communicate exclusivity, depending on the couple, though in mine it does. You just... uh, say if it does or not, really. It's like a conversation. I give it to you, you either accept it or not, and then when and if you're ready, you reciprocate. Then, when we are certain, we give it back and get pierced."[4]

Cora pursed her lips. Honestly, it made a great deal of sense. She liked that it was stating

---

4. As one can imagine, these sorts of cultural conversations have since become increasingly common, but at this, one of the earliest stages of the rebellion, they were quite groundbreaking. Cora, in her role as Head Librarian went on to introduce courses and talks about culture in order to help the disparate peoples of the Empire understand one another in ways the Pathians actively supressed.

one's own intentions and commitment, rather than asking for the same back immediately. "And if I refused to accept it?"

"It would mean that you weren't interested. That you weren't interested in seeing where things went." His voice was soft, and sad. but he gave her the option nonetheless. He still held it, his hands running over the gold chain over and over, one after the other.

"In that case, I think you have something of mine..." she whispered.

Asterion smiled, wide and welcoming, heated and hopeful in a way that made her melt. For months she'd watched him, studied him from the corner of her eyes, and never had she seen him smile like that. Like everything in the world was exactly as it should be.

"That I do... May I put it on you? Over your clothes, I mean..."

Cora nodded, somewhat nervous to have his hands on her.

Instead of walking around her back, like she expected, Asterion approached her front. The chain looked so tiny in his hands that it practically disappeared. Heat pulsed off of him, and Cora burned with it. His arms wrapped around her back, encircling her with his chain. Asterion's warm breath rustled the hairs on her head, tickling her with the reminder of his closeness. He didn't touch her as he looped the chain around her back, but she could feel how close he was, reinforced by the chain sliding against the fabric of her nightgown.

When his hands looped to the front, Cora was struck by how delicate his movements were. He had large hands with thick fingers, but he worked them deftly, looping the chain through the ring in a complex pattern that secured the thing. After, a length of chain hung down the front of her nightdress, ending just before her knees.

"We can tie that up, as well, if you'd like, but many people leave it hanging... as a reminder."

Indeed, the chain would hang low, between her legs, as she walked. If she weren't careful, when worn underneath her clothing, it would likely occasionally settle between them, nestled against her sex. She imagined going about her day, the constant reminder of him tickling and teasing her. She'd be a needy mess at the end of the day... And didn't that sound delicious?

Cora blew a slow breath out between her lips. "That would be a reminder for sure."

Asterion smiled a lot. It was ready and rarely left his face longer than a few minutes, so Cora had seen many versions of his smile. The look that came over his face then? The slow spreading of his lips in a way that dripped of satisfaction and sex? That wasn't a smile she'd ever seen but would love to see more of. He slipped a finger under the length of the chain, running it back and forth so that his finger just grazed the fabric of her nightgown.

"I suppose this is a good time to tell you that I don't mean to fight fair. I want you, Cora, and I'll fight dirty to keep you." His voice rolled through her, fanning the flames of desire that licked at her insides. Her mouth hung lax and she panted unsteady breaths.

"Fuck, Cora," he groaned, looking briefly at the ceiling as if trying to regain control of himself. "I thought you were beautiful the moment I saw you, but now? With your cheeks flushed and your hair mussed from the wind, and in a nightgown and wearing my chain? I've never seen anything I liked more."

Cora's mind flitted from thought to thought. From elation that someone seemed to see her and wanted what they saw, to nerves at the possibility of losing him. Concern at the overwhelming size of him, before she even had him, at his smell so close she could almost taste him.

Cora meant to say something smart, truly she did. Or perhaps she'd meant to say something witty. Instead, all that came out was a breathless

"Ha!" that was less a laugh than a sound of disbelief.

With that thick finger still looped through her chain, Asterion applied the slightest pressure, inviting her closer to him. Cora stumbled as if she'd been tugged, but really, she'd already been swaying with her want, and that tiny movement was all it took to send her stumbling into his chest.

With slow, almost inexorable movement, Asterion lowered his head. Strands of his hair flopped over his forehead. Breaths shaking in and out of her, Cora tried to steady herself. Surely, he would kiss her now? The slow descent of his head toward hers meant nothing else, right? He met her eyes, shifting back-and-forth between hers, as if searching for something. When he had almost closed the gap, Asterion shut his eyes and tipped his forehead against her.

He was overwhelming. The scent, the heat of him, the singular small place where the back of his finger brushed her stomach. She had experienced arousal before, but this felt deeper. It was an aching need to be touched, for connection. Because, beyond how much she wanted him to touch her, Cora craved the acceptance and connection of sharing touch with someone who truly seemed to value her for who she was.

Allowing her eyelids to flutter closed, Cora matched him, and waited. She was shocked when she first felt his touch on her forehead. He tipped his against hers and it was so beautifully, achingly intimate, but Cora worried she might cry. He was so close, it was overwhelming. Her entire body was sensitized and ready for him. Each molecule reached for him, sang for him.

Shifting his head, Asterion ran his nose against hers. She had never rubbed noses with anyone before, but as he ran the flattened warmth of his against hers, she thought, this is what love could feel like. It was only a taste, a preview of what the future could hold, but she was desperate for it.

When he spoke, Asterion's words tickled against her lips, his breath warm, and sweet. "Please, can I kiss you, Cora?"

Asterion's words scattered across her lips, across her nerves, and shattered through her. A lightning bolt, burning her to her core and rebuilding her from the ashes. It was a miracle that she was able to answer.

"Yes," she said.

Asterion nuzzled his nose against hers again. Rubbing the soft, warm and slightly furred suede expanse of his against her own. She suppressed a giggle; she didn't want him thinking that she didn't take this seriously.

Cora closed her eyes, allowing the sensations to rush over her. Asterion's warm breath, the steady, reassuring weight of his hand as it slipped around her waist. His other hand, snaking up her back to twine into her hair. And then, the delicious press of his lips against her, gentle and questing. His kiss was an invitation, a conversation. *Will you join me? Will you fall with me into something unknown and exciting?* In a dance as ancient as the very stones from which she formed, she answered. *Yes*, she said with each kiss. Yes, was the slide of her lips against his, her body melting into his embrace. Yes, was the parting of her lips and invitation for entrance.

Once invited, once accepted, Asterion was no longer timid. His tongue flowed into her mouth, inevitable and seductive. He teased her, savoring her, and she was bowled over by the sensation. His mouth tasted of the heady spices of the wine they'd shared, and she could get drunk on tasting him alone. All too soon, he was pulling away, leaving her questing with her mouth for him. Eyes closed, she searched, bereft of his warmth, overwhelmed by his absence. He didn't go far, his forehead pressed to hers again, though she could feel his shaking where he touched her.

"I need to say goodnight. I have so much to do tomorrow. I know I need to leave, but even backing up has cost me." His words were quiet, even had the library been filled, they were pitched so quiet only she would have been able to hear them. "Will I see you at the ball tomorrow? I'd offer to accompany you, but I need to be there early."

"I–I hadn't planned on–" A crowded room full of people still sounded like a nightmare... but with Asterion looking at her like she'd hung the stars, it almost sounded like a nightmare she might be willing to brave for him. "I don't have anything to wear..."

"I was hoping you'd say that." Asterion turned around and reached into the phaeton, extracting one final box from under the seat. It was wide and long, white, and tied with a golden ribbon. He pressed it into her hands and leaned in to kiss her forehead. "Think about it, for me?"

Cora watched him as he left, unable to tear her eyes away as he drove off. As soon as he was gone, however, she tore the ribbon off of the box and gasped. Lovingly wrapped in the same tissue she knew from her own modiste was an absolutely stunning gown. Her hands shook as she removed it, knowing how much such a thing would cost, and immediately seeing the thought that had gone into the design.

She hated crowds, and the thought of dancing in front of half the town made her feel like her stomach was about to drop through the floor... but the ball was something Asterion had worked *so* incredibly hard on... and the dress was really so, *so* lovely... it would be a shame to let it go to waste, wouldn't it?

Chapter Six

IN WHICH ASTERION IS NERVOUS, FRIENDS ARE INDISPENSIBLE, AND CORA IS RESPLENDENT

T HE NEXT DAY WAS so busy that Asterion shouldn't have had time to think about Cora. The problem was, he'd done nothing but think about her for months. Hell, the only way he'd been able to motivate himself to do all the crazy holiday shenanigans was to think about how happy they'd make her. And after seeing her the night before? His mind was abuzz with the possibilities of her. He'd surprised her, he knew it, and it had *all* been worth it.

Standing in the grand ballroom though, twisting his hands, he began to get nervous. What if she hated the dress? What if she realized how little he actually knew about her? What if the crowd was too much and she saw his urging to attend as a failure to understand what she would want. He knew that she'd not be excited about the crowd, but he'd hoped... well, that somehow she'd understand how much it meant to him. Somehow... without him actually telling her that.

Running a hand through his hair, he turned in a circle. Gods, he was so *stupid.* Of course she had no idea, he'd been so stunned by their kiss that he had *barely* remembered to ask her, let alone give her the dress he'd had specially made. His parents had been thrilled about his interest when he'd written, and his father had responded with a four page letter on proper courting. Obviously not *all* of the tactics would work with Cora, he couldn't kidnap and lock her in a maze of his making, in order to show her his prowess, but some had seemed worthy. Now, though? Standing in a crowded room, sweating through his one shouldered chiton? He was convinced he'd mucked things up somehow.

As ridiculous as it seemed, the fabrics he'd used were white, forest green and gold, specially chosen to suit the season, but also to best highlight Cora's beauty. He'd worried that the ball would be a step too far, but he wanted a partner, someone who would take his own work into account. He'd placed the circular tables around the edges of the room where the lights were lower in case she needed a quiet place to sit. His head whipped around the large building, ensuring that the crystals were all set to the correct hue and light levels, that none of the swags of fabric had fallen, and that none of the fresh flowers had wilted in the last five minutes.

He staggered when a large hand clapped him on the shoulder. "Nervous, 'Sterion?" Torsten was a large orc man, dressed in traditional orcish clothing, including a flat hat, known elsewhere as a beret, but he was certain they had their own name for it.[1]

Asterion coughed after the slap had knocked a bit of air from his lungs. "A bit," he admitted.

"Aw, leave him alone, Tor. It's normal, especially when the girl said she'd not be

---

1. Orcs call these hats txapelle, which can be difficult for outsiders to say, but the cap is extremely meaningful to them. As best we can tell, it is an element of Orcish culture unsullied by Pathian influence, and as such, became a symbol of their fight for freedom that they could wear even under the Empire's noses.

coming," Torsten's small wife, Catrin, chided him. The couple had had him over to dinner several times and, after finding out about his feelings for Cora, had been a great help in locating her presents. Around their feet, their two eldest children jumped up and down to get his attention.

"Asterion, look, Halsten and I match and Tilly–" Ursule, their daughter, looked around for someone.

"Their cousin is in town, and she's very excited," Catrin whispered. "Tilly is at home with the sitter tonight, remember?"

"Oh, right."

"Ah, well, you both look very smart!" And they did. The girl wore a long red skirt, in the orcish fashion, with thick black bands at the bottom, and her brother was a color coordinating version of their father. "No little one today, then?"

"Bjorn is much too young for a ball," the boy, Halsten explained. "Suley and I are mature, but he would just make a scene."

"I still made them outfits though!" Ursule piped back up, spirits apparently lifted. "They looked sooooo cute!"

A large man, who shared some features–other than the white hair and pale skin–with Catrin, walked up with a shorter woman on his arm. She wore a long, flowing dress that had large, puffy sleeves in a bright peach that offset her warm skin and deep brown hair.

"I believe you've exchanged letters with my sister-in-law, Sirin?" Catrin said, with a hand toward the woman.

Asterion started, instantly excited. "Oh yes, Sirin, it is so lovely to meet you! Thank you so much for all your help!" He grasped her hand, shaking it up and down.

"Of course! I am always happy to help please another scholar! Did she like them? Will we get to meet her?"

"I think she did... she seemed to at least, though I'm unsure if she'll be able to come tonight. I think the crowd might be—"

Young Ursule's exaggerated gasp interrupted him and they all turned to follow her gaze.

There, descending the stairs, was the woman of his dreams. Cora took the stairs slowly, her face apprehensive as she scanned the crowd. The gold pearls of her gown sparkled in the light, and Asterion's breath caught at the sight of her. He'd spent a good deal of time negotiating with her modiste on just the right style, and looking at her, she was every inch a goddess descending to earth. She'd done her hair up in twists with delicate combs and something that caught the light of the ballroom.

When her gaze swept to him, and then she smiled? Asterion's breath was stolen and his heart threatened to beat out of his chest. She was a vision. A vision that was apparently *happy* to see him. As if feeling the many eyes she'd drawn, Cora hurried down the steps. She scurried over to him, eyes frantic though she smiled and nodded her head, avoiding conversation until she grasped his arm.

Her heart beat was a tattoo against his arm, but he wasn't sure he'd ever seen as lovely a look on anyone's face as the relief that washed over hers as she grasped him. With her other hand, she pressed her hand to her cheek, which had flushed a becoming shade of pink.

There was some primal thing inside him which seeing her in clothing he'd given her satisfied. The deep red, he was pleased to see, offset the veining in her skin so that the gold shone. The golden pearls in intricate patterns of embroidery, recalled the complex natural geometries of the shells she so loved. The upper edge of the dress mimicked a seashell, scalloped along the tops of her breasts with tucks of folds that gathered to a point at her waist.

"Oh Cora!" little Ursule exclaimed. "I wanted you to see my dress, but look at *yours!* I don't think I've ever seen anything more beautiful!"

"Nor have I," Asterion said, looking down at the woman who had stolen his heart.

"I have! Just look at this cavern, Asterion, it's —well, just gorgeous!" Cora blinked, sputtering as if perhaps overwhelmed, but Cat and Torstens saved him, making introductions to their family. Cora nodded and said her hellos, all the while clinging to his arm like a lifeline. She had pretty manners, his mate, and as he scanned the room, he noticed a good many people admiring her.

Mate. He'd not yet allowed himself to think of her that way, not until he'd affixed his ring around her middle.

The thought of it, dangling between her legs, between stockinged thighs that he had wrapped in the softest gossamer silk. His mouth watered at the thought, of her wrapping those stocking clad thighs around his head, of peeling them off her to reveal her smooth, cool calves and ankles. It was no wonder her skin reflected the marble from which she'd been formed, she was as perfect as a statue. A testament, a celebration of virility and grace.

The warmth of Cora's hand left his arm and she drifted toward Sirin, hands waving as the other woman nodded.[2] Berne, Sirin's partner, caught his eye and winked. "Birds of a feather, ey?"

"I suppose so, yes," Asterion was enraptured, as he always was, when she grew excited. Her face lit up and her lips moved as if she could hardly contain them. They migrated to the side of the room when the dancing began, and Berne and Asterion took turns fetching their ladies' drinks, but it seemed they were content to talk about their passions for the whole night. Asterion would have felt neglected, if it weren't for the many small touches that Cora made, as if attempting to reassure herself he was still there. They were subtle things, a hand on his arm, leaning back into his chest, but each one sent a message. *I am comfortable because you are here*, they said. After a good six dances or so, Asterion decided it was his time. Berne nodded over his wife's shoulder as Asterion tapped on Cora's.

"Hmm?" she asked, immediately turning to him as if part of her attention had been focused on him the entire time.

---

2. At times, it is odd to write about oneself as if from an outsider's perspective, but I have also found, in my years of doing so, that it can be incredibly enlightening. Had I never written these books, for example, I might never know how meaningful our conversation was to Cora.

"I wonder, might I have this dance?"

Cora shivered and nodded. It was a waltz, so it was one of the easier dances, and Asterion was certain that even if she didn't know it, he could simply lift her up and no one would need know.

Asterion wrapped his arms around Cora, and his heart warmed at the way she leaned into him, like she was deriving strength from his presence. Her hands shook, nonetheless, her eyes frantically darting around the room.

"Eyes here, sugar plum," he said, tipping her chin up to him. "Ignore everyone else. It's just you and me here. None of them matter. This moment is for us."

The music started up, the strings of the orchestra filling the room and buoying Asterion along. Cora seemed flustered as she followed–maybe she really didn't have much dance experience–but he was able to get them started on the right foot regardless.

Her eyes never left him, and in moments, the world had shrunk for him, too. The crowd was nothing but a blur behind her as they twirled across the floor. The lighting, which he'd spent hours choosing and getting just so, no longer mattered except how it caught on the gold of her hair and the pearls on her dress.

Chapter Seven

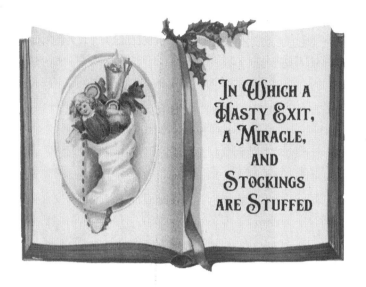

In Which a Hasty Exit, a Miracle, and Stockings are Stuffed

T HOUGH SHE'D NOT WANTED to attend this ball, what little girl didn't dream of being whisked across the floor, the envy of everyone, in the arms of some gorgeous suitor? Asterion's chiton matched the red of her dress, and there was a large, gold medallion at his shoulder depicting the crest of his people. He danced her across the floor, her feet light and effervescent in a way she'd never felt. She knew, nominally, how to waltz, she'd learned on the tops of her father's feet, and with such a confident partner, it came back to her. It wasn't easy, per se, but it was at least fun.

As Asterion led her through a turn, she could feel his chain where it hung between her legs, swinging and tickling against her. Her skirts floated around her, and she smiled, noticing the sprig of mistletoe he'd tied to his horn.

"I see even your horns are festive tonight," she teased.

"Of course!" He smiled, his ears wiggling. "It's a minotaur thing. Obviously wearing a sprig on one's horns is seen as bad form on any other night, but on Yule? We have a bit of leeway. And really, can you blame me? Very few people here actually know about the kissing tradition, but the only one I care about does."

"Does that mean you are looking for something?" All the spinning must be making her dizzy, or maybe it was simply being with Asterion. Her stomach was a mass of nerves but there, with him, everything felt just right.

On their next turn, Asterion leaned down to whisper in her ear. "Yes," he said, stealing a quick kiss on his way back.

"Very sneaky." Cora couldn't help blushing, nor the silly smile that graced her face.

When the song came to a close, Asterion bowed and she curtsied. They kept eye contact the whole time, and the giddy feeling that had been building in Cora's chest all night was fit to burst.

Asterion held out his hand for hers, and she allowed him to lead her off the dance floor. He walked back toward their friends but pulled her aside before arriving.

"With that magical moment complete, would you like to leave or stay?"

"What?" Could Asterion even leave? "Didn't you plan all of this?"

"Yes, but I also planned it knowing that you might want to leave before it was all done. At this point, it's hands off for me."

"Hands off... are you sure? Maybe your hands would really rather be otherwise occupied?"

"You little minx." Asterion lifted her, his hands sliding effortlessly under her ass and lifting her until her face was level with his. "I would like nothing more than to have them otherwise occupied, but only if you want to leave. I know this sort of thing is overwhelming for you–"

"Yes, let's leave."

Over and over, Asterion showed how well he understood her, how his time spent had truly been about observing and understanding her. She had a great deal of catching up to do, it seemed. While coming to the ball, and even dancing in front of everyone had seemed overwhelming, she'd done so because she'd wanted to show Asterion how she valued the hard work he'd done. Perhaps a ball wasn't her personal idea of a good time, but it was clear, from the happy faces around them, that this was many people's cup of tea.

They returned to their friends, Asterion cupping her hand tenderly in the crook of his arm.

"Well all, we are headed out. I have been working on this all day, and frankly I am worn out. Cora has graciously allowed me to call an end to the night."

With a round of goodbyes and hugs, they saw their way out of the party. As they ascended the grand steps at the entrance of the hall, Cora was able to take in the true beauty of everything Asterion had wrought. No longer nervous, she was able to appreciate the swags of fabric that softened the harsh cavern walls. The color-coded gemstones that shone and the sprigs of greenery that festooned nearly every surface.

"You really did a lovely job," she whispered, squeezing his hand.

"I'm glad you think so. I tried to pay attention to what decor you seemed to favor, even if you had something against mistletoe..." He smiled

out of the corner of his mouth, looking down
at her.

"In my defense... you were dangerous."

"Was I? How so?"

"Well, to my heart, I mean. And every time I
saw a sprig of it, I remembered that it seemed
a minotaur tradition and it made me think of
you."

"In that case, you were entirely right."

When they left the ballroom and ventured
into the cavern of the city proper, Cora gasped.

Soft snow was falling, *inside!* Roofs of houses
had barely a dusting, but from where they
stood, elevated on the border of the cavern, the
city sparkled with it. She held her hands up, to
catch the flakes on her hand. She looked up at
the cavern ceiling in wonder, half expecting it
to be gone entirely. But no, instead, soft clouds
rolled across the roof. A steady fall of snow
descended. Asterion tugged her hand to the
side, tilting his horns for her to look.

Sitting on a balustrade that led to the
ballroom entrance was another nymph. This
one seemed male, and he had a smirk on his
face, very aware that she was watching. Sparkles
extended from the hand he casually gestured
with, a current of snow magic flowing from
him to the clouds above. Like her, he had white
skin, though his own hair was white as well.

Perhaps she should have been confused about his nature, having never seen him, or really any other nymph before, but she felt an instinctive, tangible kinship to him. On sight, she knew he was a nymph, and knew that he was tied to the element of snow.

"You truly thought of everything, didn't you?" she asked. Her voice was barely a whisper, thick with emotion. While she could experience snow on outcroppings of her mountain, she'd never seen Berggeheimnis look so beautiful. While others could visit other places and experience the joy of a magical walk through town in the snow, she had assumed it was just one more thing denied to her based on her nature.

"Cora, I want to give you everything, not just the things that you think you deserve. Everything."

"I don't know about *everything*, but I am certainly excited to see what you come up with, especially if this is the result!"

Asterion whisked her up into his arms, clopping down the steps and onto the street below. When they arrived on level ground, he spun them in a circle, smiling like a giddy boy. "He said that in the morning, there should be enough to make snowmen!"

Cupping his cheeks, Cora pulled his face toward hers, fingers snaking up to his horn to tousle the mistletoe he'd tied there. Their lips fit together so easily, so perfectly aligned, that it was hard not to read into what it might mean. Asterion's kisses were like long pulls of wine, complex and warming her through, drugging her deeper with each taste.

"Will you make one with me?" she whispered when they separated, heat pooling in her core as he surrounded her. "In the morning, I mean?"

"Of course, we could meet up early outside of the library and surprise the patrons!"

"No, I mean, well, yes that is a lovely idea, but I was sort of hoping that we wouldn't need to meet up…"

Asterion's eyes went wide with realization. "Oh! Yes, that would be even better. Obviously…" His ears wiggled, which might just be Cora's new favorite of his expressions.

He lifted her and took off walking toward her home at a quick pace. "I can walk, you know!"

"Yes, but your legs are shorter. It will be faster this way."

"Is 'faster' your main concern then?"

"If seeing the inside of your bedroom is what is at the end of the trip, then yes."

"My bedroom? You don't want to go to yours?" Her bed wasn't exactly sized for a minotaur, nor was she sure if he would fit through her doorways without needing to duck.

"Yours is closer. Plus, that way we won't have to travel across the city to get to the library in the morning."

He was apparently quite serious about making those snowmen in the morning.

Her house was indeed close by, as the library and the ballroom were both located in one of the cultural hubs. As they approached the great, two-story edifice of the library, Asterion slowed.

"Do you really not close the doors?" he asked, referencing the large stone doors that could be pulled shut to protect the two-story glass windows and smaller entrance doors.

"Can you imagine me trying to close them? Trust me, I've tried. They are much too heavy for me."

"Well, I assume I can help with that." His head was tilted to the side as if in thought.

"I never thought it mattered much. The library is for everyone, what does it matter if they can see inside after hours?"

"It will matter if I am ever to fuck you on one of those study tables." He said it so nonchalantly, and then he blushed deep red, ears wiggling again. "I mean, well..."

"Have you thought about that, then?" She raised an eyebrow. Normally, such a thing would likely have appalled her–think how *messy* it would be in her library–but she was hard pressed to deny the appeal of it.

"More often than you might think." He dipped his head and looked away from her.

"Well then, I think I should happily accept your help at some point... but today I think you wanted to see where I slept?"

Asterion lowered his head to hers and pressed his soft lips on her forehead. "Yes, please."

Asterion allowed her to walk as they approached her door, and she pulled out her crystal to place it against the lock. There was a small click as the lock released and allowed her to push the door open. Her home was dark for the time being, but her lamps flared to life as she turned on the gas and lit the pilot light near the door.

"Here we are then, though I suppose you already knew where I lived." She wrung her hands in front of her and turned around, rocking on her toes.

The lintel was indeed too low, and Asterion had to duck to get inside. It was almost comical, watching this hulking beast of a man bend himself in half to come through her doorway. Once inside, though, she was pleased to see that he still had several inches of clearance above his head. Despite the clearance, he was obviously still *large*. The walls were close around him and Cora could scarcely believe that she'd nearly forgotten how much bigger he was than her.

He didn't seem to mind, though. His eyes held fast to her and the only way she could describe the look on his face was hungry. Here was a man ready to devour her. Asterion's chest heaved, eyes dilated and he huffed a breath out of his nose. She'd never really appreciated his nose before, but now, staring at her like a man starved and with his ring hanging between her legs, teasing the lips of her pussy? She could just imagine where it would pierce through. It would hang there, under his nose, marking him as hers for all the world to see... and she couldn't wait.

Though he looked seconds from bursting into action, Asterion drew in a deep breath and rolled his shoulders. He raised his hands and pressed them against the walls on either side of him. The action seemed to ground him, because his breathing leveled and when he opened his eyes, they still held desire, but it was one he now held the reins of.

"I like your house." It was a simple statement, but his body language went beyond. His thick fingers roamed over the stone walls, trailing along as he walked toward her. "The walls... they are nice and close, and I can't see what's beyond this corridor. It's good."

"I'm glad. The uh, parlor is through there and–" Cora squeaked at Asterion lifted her and pressed her at the back wall of the hall where it split into a T.

"Sugar plum, I am certain the parlor is lovely, but I am sure I won't remember a thing about it. I'm in *your* home. Everything smells like you, and for the first time in over a year, I feel properly walled in. My chain is hanging between your legs, you're wearing the dress that I designed while choking my cock thinking about you, and gods help me, these thighs..." he squeezed them for good measure. "These fucking thighs are wrapped in the finest gossamer silk I could find, and I am afraid I will destroy them. So, if you don't mind, do you think you could show me your bedroom first?"

Heat pulsed through Cora from every place where Asterion touched her. Had anyone ever been so affected by her as Asterion?

Had *she* ever been so affected?

She was a nymph, after all, and no stranger to sexual desire, but this was the first time that she felt true, genuine care from a potential partner, and it only stoked her higher. Emboldened, she leaned forward and captured his lips with hers once more. There was an urgency to his kiss this time, a desperation that was certainly flattering.

Grabbing his horns, Cora tugged in the direction of her bedroom, and Asterion, bless him, followed her direction. He held her against him with one hand, while the other explored the back of her dress. It had buttons, round and flat, instead of the more ornamental buttons she would have expected. They hadn't required a button looper for her to get on, nor had she needed assistance, thank the Lady. Because of this, her dress easily fell away from her shoulders, draping down her front to reveal her ivory satin chemise and frilly, special occasion, stays. Asterion hooked his hoof underneath the dress and tossed it up into his hand, muttering about how "pretty things don't belong on the ground

As they neared her room, however, Cora felt anxiety rise in her chest. Her room wasn't exactly... normal, she'd learned in the past. And though she'd already decided, before the ball, that she'd like to bring him back, she had

entirely failed to make it seem any more...
normal.

Before she had much time to think about
it, though, they tumbled through her doorway
and Asterion released her to bounce down onto
her bed.

He towered over her, entirely too big for
her bed, and took her in with wild eyes. The
lights were low, but several deep breaths later,
he seemed to center himself enough to look
around the room. Cora was torn between
squeezing her eyes shut and watching his
reaction, so she settled for turning beet red and
peeking out from between her fingers.

At first glance, her room did, in fact, appear
quite normal. She had a large canopy bed
swathed in thick red curtains, and a few
select pieces of furniture. Further inspection,
however, revealed the humanoid depression
in the wall where she could retreat into her
mountain when she needed the pressure and
quiet. According to others, though, it was
highly odd. The true thing that had made
others uncomfortable, and her self-conscious,
in the past, was her collection of toys that sat
above her bed.

Sculpted crystal phalluses and teasers lined
the shelf above where she slept, ready to be
retrieved at a moment's need, but outright

beautiful of their own volition. She loved the array of sizes and shapes, colors and textures.

Asterion took it all in, his head cocking in curiosity when he looked at her depression. When he saw the head of her bed, however, his eyes widened... in interest?

Asterion licked his lips, and did his ears wiggle? Yes, he lowered his head, perhaps blushing a bit, but obviously interested.

"You've got quite the collection," he observed.

"I've been alone for a long time."

"You'll have an even bigger one now that you aren't."

And there it was. *That* was truly the essence, the perfection of Asterion. He didn't question who she was, because–wonder of wonders–he *liked* who she was.

"Will I, now?" she asked.

"I don't think it's any surprise that I like spoiling you, Sugar Plum. And I like spoiling your pussy best of all."

He knelt at the end of the bed, licking his lips, his eyes flicking between her and her toys as if torn. "I'll have to investigate those further at some point, but let's get back to the subject at hand. My favorite subject. You."

Leaning over, he reached beside her to grab a pillow. Lifting her head, he slipped it underneath.

Cora could not have feigned disinterest if she tried. Her mouth hung open and her eyes tracked his every movement as if her life depended on it. She gasped when he cradled her foot in his thick palm, lifting it, and her slipper, so gently, so reverently, that it made her breath stutter. With those same, worshipful hands, he slipped behind her back, untying her skirts and sliding them down the bed beneath her. Cora took the opportunity to unlace her stays, allowing them to flop down onto the bed on either side of her. Asterion snapped his hungry eyes back to her, licking his lips and devouring the soft mounds of her breasts outlined in the thin fabric.

Asterion draped her dress over a chair set at the corner of her room and placed her foot on his chest, nestled between his pectoral muscles, teasing the edge of his chiton. He slipped a finger inside and tickled her arch with a wicked smile before sliding it off. Cora squirmed, giggling.

With her slipper placed gently on the floor beside him, Asterion glided his hands up her calf. He met her gaze, watching her every reaction, as if ensuring that all was well. The scrutiny stole her breath and made her heart flutter. His large hands reverently consumed each inch of her flesh until he'd pushed her chemise up to reveal her thighs. In addition to the dress, he'd also included a set of stockings so paper thin she could feel each minute shift of his hands on her. At the top, they were scalloped, mimicking the pattern of her dress, though not beaded.

Asterion licked his lips, as if she were a meal to be consumed.

"I hoped I'd be able to see your veins through them," he whispered. He traced one such vein of gold with his finger, as if mapping the path to her heart and her pleasure. Then, with a gentle tug, he began rolling the thin fabric down her thighs and lowered his head to trace the same vein of gold with his lips. His kisses were brief and soft, teasing rather than consuming. He lavished her with attention, and when he reached her foot and pulled the stocking off, both of them were flushed and breathing heavily.

"I can't tell you how often I dreamed of these legs," he whispered against her other leg, where he was poised to repeat the process.

Cora shook her head, it was more than she could have ever imagined. The soft caresses across her skin, the tender words, and most importantly, the disbelieving expressions he kept giving to match her own. *This* was everything. Someone who truly seemed to believe themselves as lucky as she did when it came to being with her. It was what she'd always wanted. It was what she'd always deserved.

Tears pricked at her eyes, and she blinked them back. No, she would not become overwhelmed in this moment, she would not allow herself to be overcome with emotion. She *needed* to be here. To feel all the tender acceptance in Asterion's touch.

Once both of her stockings lay draped across her dress, Asterion returned his hands between her legs, his eyes focused, strangely, along the end of the bed, rather on her. She didn't need to wait long to see what he was looking at though, because she felt the chain move against her core when Asterion picked it up. He rolled the delicate chain between his blunt fingers, a slow smile spreading across his face. Even with just that, the small twists of it tickled the front of her chemise and sent fissions through where it teased her clit.

"I'm beginning to see the appeal of these chains," she panted.

"This chain is gorgeous, but I'd rather see it against your skin." His hands tracked higher, but Cora was pulsing with need and had no time or patience for his slow exploration. Instead, she stood, putting the chain, and his ring, level with his face, and whipped her chemise over her head. Her nipples pebbled at the sensation and then she was completely exposed to him.

Wide hands grasped her hips and Asterion's thumbs toyed with the chain on either side of his ring. His gaze seemed riveted there, thumbs and eyes fixated on the chain that claimed her. Asterion tipped his head back, his tousled hair falling away from his forehead. Asterion tucked his thumbs underneath the chain and slid it up her body, until they teased the undersides of her breasts.

"I—" Asterion shook his head, though he was careful with his horns. "I never thought we'd actually get here. That you'd be wearing my chain."

He sniffled, and his eyes were watery when he next met her gaze. How could a man this beautiful ever think such a thing?

"Truly? Asterion, you are—perfect? How could I do anything but end up here, with you? I was already half in love with you, though I would never have admitted it, when you started this magical scenario."

"Well, I do love that..." He ran the tip of a finger along the underside of her breast, making her shiver.

Cora gasped, as the rush of sensation heightened. She buried her hands in his hair and breathed deep. The mistletoe, tied on his horn, caught her eye, and she slipped it off the top. She lowered it, so that it was between them, and twirled the spring.

"So, this mistletoe..." she started, feeling bold. "What if I held it, say... here?" She moved it until the clipping hung over her nipple. "You'd have to kiss me there?"

Asterion didn't bother answering, instead, he leaned forward and pulled it into his mouth, sucking and toying with it until she arched against him. He released her only to show the other the same level of care and Cora couldn't hold back the moan of desire that released from her lips.

"That's the idea. Though, now you've given me another." With a smirk, he snatched the mistletoe from her hand and wrapped his arms around her, lifting and pulling her until she was fully on the bed.

She giggled as she bounced down. When she opened her eyes, Asterion was unlatching the shoulder of his chiton. It fell off his shoulder and down to the ground to pool at his feet. Cora could hardly believe her eyes. Just as he'd said, and so constrained it was nearly purple, was Asterion's cock. She'd expected it to be large, of course, he was so much bigger than her, but she hadn't understood the implications of their prior conversation.

Indeed, he'd lashed his cock to his leg, the bulbous head an angry deep purple. She frowned because it actually looked fairly painful, and she was annoyed on his behalf.

He chuckled. "It's normally not like this. Usually, I am used to it, but today I think this situation is understandable." Asterion grimaced as he unwound the length of leather, and his cock leaped back up to what she presumed was its normal position as soon as it was released.

Without the leather constraining it to his leg, Cora allowed herself to take in what he looked like. He was long and wide, with a prominent swell midway down his shaft. When he pulled foreskin back, Cora could see a glint of metal on the underside of his head.

He stood next to the bed, and Cora was certain that he was about to hold the sprig over his cock, it's what she would have done of course, but instead he picked her up so that she straddled him and turned to lay on the bed. She sat atop him now, and the faint warmth of his shaft just barely teased at her ass. He dangled the mistletoe between them, as she had, and moved it so that it was over his mouth.

He was smiling when she bent over to kiss him, loving the soft expanse of his skin beneath her. He was lightly furred, with hair so short that it was barely detectable. It didn't appear as if he would grow a beard as a dwarf might, but Cora liked that he was so different from everyone she'd ever known.

While they kissed, Asterion dragged the mistletoe up Cora's arm, toying with her heightened feeling. He traced it across her back and around her neck, circled each breast, and when he teased it right above the golden curls of her sex, she was writhing with need.

"Well, I can hardly reach to kiss there," she teased.

"No, but I can." Asterion dropped the mistletoe over the side of the bed and grasped her thighs. With ridiculous ease, he lifted her forward so that her knees were on either side of his head, and her pussy hovered over his face.

"Now, it's time for *my* present, Sugar Plum." His eyes left hers, drawn first to her cunt, and then closing in bliss when he settled her over him and inhaled.

Asterion didn't bother with tentative licks, he dove straight in, sucking on her labia and licking up her slit as if every taste gave him sustenance.

"I really hope you like this, because I am going to want to eat this pussy every day," he gasped against her.

Cora would certainly have no complaints because it was like nothing she'd ever experienced. Asterion licked and suckled, teasing her clit and lapping up every bit of wetness she produced as if it were the font of all that was good in the world. As if he wasn't seeking her pleasure, but reveling in his own. Cora gasped and moaned, and it wasn't long before she was rocking above him, grinding down onto his face to chase sensation.

Asterion tore himself away from her cunt, his face glistening. "Look at that pretty pussy. No wonder you like shells so much, with her perfect pearl, she's the most beautiful thing I've ever seen." He licked up the side of her folds, savoring her between words. "Now hold on Sugar Plum. Horns..."

Cora was only too happy to oblige. She wrapped her hands around his horns and Asterion let out the most delicious growl in response.

"Oh fuck!" Cora couldn't hold back her cries. With her hands around his horns, Asterion sucked her relentlessly, demanding her pleasure as much as coaxing it.

When she neared her peak, Asterion concentrated his efforts on her clit, increasing his suction and humming. A shift of his hands was all the warning she got before Asterion flipped her onto her back. Suddenly, she was staring at the ceiling as Asterion thrust two of those thick fingers into her, curling them and lapping at her clit.

Cora bowed off the bed, every muscle in her body taut as her orgasm rippled through her. Like the waves that, had she concentrated, she could feel lapping at the shores of her mountain, so too did the pleasure that ran through her. Asterion eased her through it, prolonging her orgasm with each curl of his fingers.

When Cora lay limp and sated on the bed, Asterion pulled back, licking his lips and fisting his cock.

"Can I fill you now?"

"Please," Cora mewled, lifting her hips toward him.

"You never need to beg me for anything, love. But, I have to admit you do look pretty doing it."

He was true to his word and didn't make her wait. In a breath, his cockhead was nestled against her opening, already straining for entrance.

"You're so big." Cora wasn't sure if it was a benediction or a complaint, but it was true. Taking him would be a trial, but she wanted him inside her so desperately that she was prepared for whatever it took.

With slow, steady movements, Asterion eased himself into her, breaching her with increasing pressure. Getting past the wide lip of his head, brought relief just when she needed it, and allowed her to enjoy the bump of his piercing as it slid inside. The stretch of him was glorious, she'd never felt so full in all her life, not even when stuffing herself with two toys. He slid into her, and stopped at the thick swell of his shaft, panting as he checked in with her. "How are you doing, gorgeous?"

"Wonderful," she breathed. It was a stretch, but she *was* a nymph after all, and perhaps those stories about them being extra pliable were true because she probably *should* have been in pain, but there wasn't even a twinge. There was pressure, *so* much pressure, and it was overwhelming, but she'd expect having all your dreams come true to be overwhelming.

At first, he pumped in and out of her, gently working her onto the second swell of his cock. Cora moaned through it, each thrust breaking her open until she felt entirely exposed to him. Her mouth fell open and she keened. Asterion surrounded her, consumed her, and filled her to the brim. He leaned back on his knees, gaze fixed on where they were fused.

"Oh, fuck," he moaned. His hand flew to
her stomach, twining one finger into her ring.
"Look at you, wrapped in my chain, stuffed full
of my cock."

Cora looked down and was surprised to see
that her stomach bulged where he filled her, the
distinct outline of his cock highlighted just how
obscenely large he was compared to her.

Asterion placed his other hand on her
stomach, over where he bulged out of her, his
mouth hanging open. "I never knew this was
possible."

Pulling back, they watched as the mound
went away and reappeared when he slid home
once more. With each piston of his hips,
Asterion cemented their bond, the look of awe
on his face capturing Cora's heart.

Nervous in spite of her wonder, Cora's hand
shook as she lowered it to feel. When she did,
she moaned. She could feel as he filled her up,
even the distinct swell of his cockhead inside
her. Asterion covered her hand with his and
locked eyes with her.

In that moment, time stood still, and Cora
had no question in her mind that they were
meant to be together. With his other hand,
Asterion dragged his chain across her clit,
teasing her pearl with every thrust. Air huffed
out of his nostrils and he frowned, as if in

concentration. Releasing her hand, Asterion wrapped his hands around her hips, lifting her ass in the air and teasing her clit with his thumb. He bit down on his lips, working them.

"One more, Sugar Plum, I know you can give me one more," he growled.

She could certainly give him one more, and she was quickly approaching her orgasm, but it was his next word that sent her over the edge.

"Please," he whined. Knowing Asterion rode the edge of holding back his orgasm, that he was *trying* to wait for her, and was about to fail, was so erotic that she didn't stand a chance.

"Yes!" she screamed. "Oh, fuck yes!"

She clamped down around his cock, her orgasm squeezing him tight, and in seconds he fucked her once, twice, and was roaring as he held her firm and spurted his hot cum inside her.

Asterion shook as he came down, leaning over to kiss Cora tenderly.

He rolled them onto their sides, held her close and toyed with her chain again. "Thank you, you are the best Yule gift I've ever gotten," he whispered.

"Thank *you*. And happy holidays, Asterion."

"The first of many, Sugar Plum."

Chapter Eight

IN WHICH
FRESHLY
FALLEN SNOW
USHERS IN A
MAGICAL
MORNING

WHEN CORA WOKE, SHE was deliciously warm. Living in a mountain meant warmth that she didn't actively work for rarely happened. If she woke up in the morning and it was warm, it was because she'd gotten up to stoke the fire. As such, waking up with Asterion curled around her was deliciously decadent. His arms wrapped around her from behind, tucking her close so that her entire back was touching him in some way. One furry leg was thrown over her own, and the rest of his heat permeated the blankets. As far as she could tell, he was still asleep, his warm breaths ruffling her hair in an even cadence.

She closed her eyes, deciding to fall back to sleep for a bit longer, when the sounds of children laughing filtered through her window. Their cries of joy drew her out of bed in a flash as she remembered the magic of the previous night's snow.

She ran to the window, throwing open the sash. A puff of snow flew off of her window frame and sprinkled to the ground below. It was no longer falling, but a thick layer covered the entire city. Several children played below her window, in front of the library. Snowballs flew through the air and occasionally hit their marks, though several children were building snowmen.

Cora felt Asterion before she heard him. His arms slipped around her, and he settled his head atop hers.

"They beat us to the snow," he said.

"I think you are right, but I was apparently quite content to keep sleeping."

He grunted a response that didn't entirely sound like words.

Cora raised a brow and turned in his arms. "Are you not a morning person?"

"No, I am not, so come back to bed." He picked her up and walked back toward to lay her down.

"Asterion!" she giggled. "The window is still open!"

Pulling the covers over them, Asterion wrapped her tightly. "I am not sure what you think we are going to *do* right now, but I intend on sleeping."

"Really? I doubt that."

"Do you dare question my honor? You think I would lie about such a serious topic?" He had put on a snotty voice that sounded shockingly like the city's head councilor.

"Not exactly, I just assumed that you wanted to play again..."

"I do, but I have fantasized too often about waking up grinding my cock into your ass to miss the opportunity now."

"That is a compelling point. I will do my best to fall asleep then."

"If not, just wake me up." Asterion tucked her head under his chin and was snoring within moments. Cora reached out to her mountain, checking in as she hadn't done in days.

The mountain sent back calm contentment, which mirrored her own, and somehow included the sentiment that having snow *inside* was fun, though it was confused as to how it happened.

"Magic," she whispered. "One magical minotaur set on creating a fantasy."

"Just for you," Asterion mumbled. "Always for you."

Want to know more about that orca shifter
and selkie in the library? Read about them this
February in the Rake! When our rakish orca
is looking for a snack, he never expects that
instead he'll bind himself to a selkie and lose his
heart in the process. Aegir's book is next, and
we'll make our first forays into the Empire and
flip the traditional seklie lore on it's head, until
we're wondering, who captured who...
Pre-order now on Amazon!

THE RAKE
OR
THE ORCA WHO MET HIS MATCH
IN A SELKIE DESIRING REVENGE
BY:
KASS O'SHIRE

https://www.amazon.com/dp/B0CSPRDRRH

Kass is a reluctant human living in America's own little Shire. Kass uses she/her pronouns and is both is demi and bi. Her writing focuses on body, sex, and equality positive stories with high heat levels and cozy vibes. She loves monster romance/paranormal romance, gas-lamp fantasy romance, historical romance, sci-fi romance (ok, all things romance), epic fantasy and space opera. In her free time, she reads a lot, bakes her pants off, and plays and DMs DnD and other tabletop and board games. She's married to a pretty great guy who is convinced he is Berne (he's not), has one awesome 13 year old son and has done two surrogacies for the most amazing couple. To pay the bills, Kass is a data analyst in mental and behavioral health. As a result, she's extremely passionate about access to care for all folks. As you could probably guess from the footnotes, she's a HUGE nerd ;)

The best place to hear things before ANYONE is Kass's Patreon! There, even free members find out juicy bits before the public, and she's better at updating it than her newsletter. Paid patrons get free ARCS, access to spicy art, the enire backlog of her extras and epilogues, sneak peeks as to what is coming next, bi-annual mailings of goodies and even book boxes and merch! Sign up now to stay in touch! patreon.com/kassoshire

You can find Kass ALL THE PLACES via her Carrdhttps://kassoshire.carrd.co/(Generally patreon, discord and insta will get you the most up to date info!)

Acknowledgements

MY ALPHA AND BETA **readers, Melissa H and Emma:** Thank you for your extremely helpful feedback, but perhaps most importantly, your encouragement. This was a super fast turnaround time and am just SO grateful for your contributions in the form of footnotes and additions.

My amazing artists FallnSkye, PhantomDame, Aliiwa, and Koijix: You inspire me every day, and I am so grateful for the stunning art you produce on my behalf.

My ARC readers: As I write this, you are actively pointing out typos to save my butt, tagging me in good reviews, letting me ignore some not so good ones, screaming at me in my dms and helping me hold it together. A post or message from one of you raises my spirits for hours or days and is more motivating than a post from me might be for a potential reader. Thank you for all you have done and will do for me and other authors. Special thanks to Cindy, Erin, Whitney, Melissa, Monica, Tieraney, and Amber.

My Amazing Sprint Partners and Peers: I am so lucky to have you. Someday I'll hug you all in person. The MonRom and Gaslamp communities are just FULL of amazing people and I am so obsessed with all of you!

Lexi: Working with you on edits has been a dream. Your feedback has been so helpful and I am so grateful for all of your little notes!

Torri: You are the reason I will always tell people to meet their internet friends. There is something so powerful about being friends with someone based on shared interests instead of proximity. Thanks for listening to me blather for hours about this book and all of the lore, can't wait to do it some more! Thank you for laughter and tears, silly boardgames and letting me steal your babies.

Tori: I cannot thank you enough for your friendship, your love, and your constant support. Also, thanks for not strangling me when I am a disorganized chaos goblin... again.

Bex: You're the Bext. We're growing and healing and I am more grateful than ever for your friendship. You make me look so good in public and I can't thank you enough.

Chris: Thanks for all you do. 12/10 husband. Thanks for jumping feet first into the world of monsterfuckery with me. I love you more than I can possibly express and I'm literally so obsessed with you it's unreal. My biggest wish is that everyone could have a partner as loving, supportive and understanding as you.

You taught me that real men can be just as good as book boyfriends, but feel free to transform into a monster at any time.

Finally, you, my reader: Thank you for spending time with me, Asterion and Cora. I cannot express how magical it is to know that people might be enjoying my silly little world. If I provided you with a little bit of joy, comfort or coziness, I am incredibly grateful for the opportunity.

She has everything she needs for a solo trek through the Arctic: a sledge heaped with supplies, a little magic, and evidently, the eye of a polar bear shifter–who shouldn't even *exist*.

Sirin is determined to find the source of magic, and nothing is going to stop her. Not expulsion from her guild, not their warnings about her "certain death," and certainly not the damned polar bear stalking her through the taiga.

Berne is a simple bear. He likes spending time shifted, a good meal, and apparently, round little scientists. When his duty to protect a thousand-year-old secret is tested against the strange pull he feels toward her, Berne can't help but sink his teeth into the one solution that might let him keep his adorable prey.

For fans of determined plus-sized heroines and cinnamon-roll bear shifters, *A Polar Expedition: and Other Stimulating Research Opportunities* is the first standalone novella in The Shades of Sanctuary, where the vibes are cozy, the heat is high and the mates are monstrous. Grab a cup of tea and snuggle in, because while the burn might be slow, the HEA is only a few hours away!

Read the book that started it all, at https://books2read.com/polar-expedition!

Stealing some horses from a magical fortress should be easy after raising twins and enduring two weeks with the orc that broke her heart.

Catrin's half-orc children are going through a difficult... growing phase. But since their orcish father left while she was pregnant, she doesn't know how to help. When Torsten, the first orc to break her heart, swaggers back into her life, he's got all the answers she needs.

Torsten has always regretted what happened with his best friend's sister when they were kids, but he had no choice. After fifteen years away, he's returned with no direction, no ties, and every reason to explore where they went wrong. A ridiculous horse heist might just be the perfect time to figure out what he wants in life... and it might involve an adorable rabbit-shifter and her orcish children. After all she's suffered, Catrin can't weather another heartbreak, but can she afford to miss out on a second chance at true love?

For fans of plus-sized heroines and golden retriever orcs, On the Care and Keeping of Orcs is the second standalone in The Shades of Sanctuary, where the vibes are cozy, the heat is high and the mates are monstrous. Grab a cup of tea and snuggle in, because while there might be some angst along the way, the burn is fast, the stakes are low, and the HEA is only a few hours away!

Read Kass's sweet, dirty talking orc at https://books2read.com/careandkeepingforcs!

The Curious Incident of the Great Cookie Snackcident of 979 is a cozy, slower burn workplace romance with two MCs who connect over a shared passion for their calling. It features a demi heroine, a non-binary shadow monster, wooing with snacks, footnotes from an in world narrator, and shadow tentacle play! If you are looking for a sexy version of the pottery scene from Ghost... this is the place to be.

Read this sweet workplace romance https://books2read.com/snack!

Made in United States
Troutdale, OR
12/16/2024

26499185R00082